MURDER, MYSTERY ARE THE

WHITBY ROCK

A NOVEL

KEV FREEMAN

To my family of adventurous creatives
Deanna, Anisha, Ellissa and Lukas

Cover Design by MiblArt

Whitby Rock a Novel
Copyright © 2021 Kev Freeman

ISBN: 978-1-7365709-0-6 (paperback)
ISBN: 978-1-7365709-1-3 (hardback)
ISBN: 978-1-7365709-2-0 (e-book)

A tale that involves a synchronicity that weaves through time and distance towards a common destination. For transparency, the threads may not have the same origin, and as stories happen, they may not lead towards a familiar end. Nonetheless, they incorporate events sewn throughout the tapestry of history and known to many.

Maybe you can remember.

1
BELFRY

*The evil spirits that be in proximity doubt their
influence when they hear the bells ringing; thus, when
angels observe such engagement through evil, or when
great thunder or heavy darkness abounds; the bells
ring to deter the wicked spirits and to dismiss them to
abandon and flee their present actions.*

The Golden Legend of the Saints,
Jacobus de Voragine, 1483.

Throughout all the named civilized ages the sound of
a church bell has been a signal of worship, of celebration,
of remembrance. A powerful harmonic vibration used to
ward off demons and evil. Now, although the air was free
from thunder and darkness, it was too late to issue a warning
to the wicked spirits circulating within the ether.

On Sunday, March 12th, 1998, a lone bell tolled with random
rhythm and had been doing so for half an hour or perhaps
more. Unrelenting, the sound from the open bronze mouth
resonated through the early morning air. It drove birds from
their roost to circle the spire of St. Bridget's church and the

cross at its peak. The large crucifix held onto the day's first rays with a golden glow. A rising sun, low on the horizon, forced the cross to cast its elongated shadow onto the grounds of Sneaton Thorpe, a village near Whitby in England.

Reverend John Coombs, the vicar of this parish for fifteen years, had called police in a panic to attend the church and to deal with what he found inside. The cause of the ringing bell. He had seen nothing like it before. Coombs stood beside the open chapel door in a state of agitation, praying and awaiting help. The first officer to attend was PC Jim Johnstone, a twenty-three-year veteran of the force. It had only taken him five minutes to reach the scene. He was the community police officer assigned to this rural area for the last four years. A likeable man who enjoyed his food, he took time to get to know the people of the village; it kept the crime rate low and his job easy.

It was a fortunate thing that he had been patrolling nearby when the call came over the radio. Inside his car he sang along to the 'The Jam's A Town Called Malice' as it played on his portable MP3 player, the headphones strapped to his head, but covering his left ear only. He should not have the music on, but sometimes, on a long shift, he did. His right ear engaged the crackling of the police radio as it interrupted the song. He threw off the headphones towards the rear seat and picked up the radio handset, slowed the car and listened.

"Whiskey four-one, Whiskey four-one. Control. Over."

"Control. This is Whiskey four-one, Go ahead over." Said Johnstone.

"Whiskey four-one. Report of break-in and possible suicide. Location: St. Bridget's Church, Sneaton Thorpe. Crime team on route. Secure the scene. Acknowledge. Over."

"Control. Will do. Will be there in fifteen minutes. Will report back when I arrive, over."

"Whisky four-one. Received. Thank you. Out."

A suicide, that meant a body, this unexpected event could prove to be interesting. Then he thought again, an unpleasant realization. Johnstone's night shift should end in fifteen minutes at 7 a.m. and his pre-ordered full English breakfast awaited him in his regular café, close to the quay car park in the nearby town of Whitby. He would be late for his meal, and he was hungry, more than that, he was starving. His belly imagined the bacon, tomato, eggs, sausage, and black pudding, ready and waiting, and issued a customary growl at the thought.

Officer Johnstone's mood darkened when he considered that the crime team were on their way and they would likely keep him around while they did all the good stuff. His task would be to secure the scene and take notes, and that would be it. All the work and no reward. Even worse, he knew that by the time he had completed his task, his breakfast would be cold. There was no saving it now.

As Johnstone arrived at the church only five minutes after the call, Reverend Coombs ran to the vehicle before its motion had stopped, his white cotton robe flowing behind him like the wings of a flightless angel. The police car came to a halt beside the entrance to the churchyard. As it did, Coombs hurled himself at the vehicle, pounding with both hands on the driver's window.

"Oh, a terrible thing, inside, an awful sight, a poor man, he is in there, hanging!"

"Steady on there, Reverend. Let me get out of the vehicle first." Said Johnstone, squeezing his ample frame between the car door and the steering wheel and forcing the Reverend to take a step backwards. Johnstone stood beside the vehicle, readjusted his tie, and placed his cap in position on his head, twisting and pulling it to a snug fit with both hands.

"Now, good morning Reverend, I think we have met before? I am PC Johnstone. So. Nice and calm tell me what is going on then?" Johnstone unbuttoned his top pocket and removed his field notebook. A small black notebook which folded along its top edge. This was the first time he had used it all week. He skipped past the report of a loose dog worrying sheep and turned to a new page. He took out his pencil and pressed the sharp tip against his tongue to lubricate the writing point. Coombs continued to talk.

"Yes, you need to go inside, to the bell tower, on the left. There is a man hanging. I think he is dead. Good Lord knows how he got up there!"

"OK, let me take your details first, Reverend, it is Coombs? Yes? Then I will look inside the chamber. Is there anyone else in there?"

"No, no-one else, Yes, I am Reverend Coombs, John."

"That is with a double 'O'?"

"Yes, officer."

"Oh, and when did you discover the incident?"

"Well, I first heard the bell sound at around 6:25 this morning."

"And were where you?"

"I was at the vicarage, just up the street. Minutes away. Having my breakfast."

Officer Johnstone's belly growled at the mention of food, it wanted to know more detail. With no acknowledgement of the gurgle, he moved on to the next question.

"You say he is dead?"

"Yes, there is no sign of life in him. He did not answer or move at all."

"How long did it take you to get over here from when you first heard the bell?"

"Only about five minutes."

"And you did not see anyone else, no vehicles?"

"No, no-one, nothing."

"All right, you need to stay here, I will check inside, do not let anyone else in unless it is the investigative team, they should arrive soon. Will you be OK?" Said Johnstone. He wrote the details in his notebook with his pencil as he spoke, then looked up to see a few villagers gathered close by the entrance to the church graveyard. Johnstone gestured to them to stay back.

"Yes, I will be OK." Said the Reverend.

Satisfied that the Reverend would stay at the door, Johnstone looked up at the spire and the circling birds and then entered the church. His footsteps produced a sharp echo as the steel segs inserted into the soles of his boots hit the stone flags of the nave. He continued through the wooden pews, with neat stacks of hymn books at their ends, to the bell ringing chamber on the west side of the building. The bell sounded, but now less regular and with a lower volume.

2
PENDULUM

The main chapel area led to the bell chamber, a stone tower supporting the church spire, the belfry and its three companion bells. The sound expanded and vibrated in his head as PC Johnstone entered the confined space. He stopped, removed his cap, and held it by his side while he ruffled his hair with his free hand, before gazing upwards towards the belfry. Johnstone's pupils widened. The darkness in the chamber broken only by the projection of a solitary sunbeam into the void through a small opening in the east wall. Small specks of dust caught dancing in the light floated in and out of focus. Johnstone, expanding his cheeks to capacity until they released their content, exhaled a puff of air. The fog of his exhaled breath swirled and caught in the cold, twisting, and morphing before him like a phantom.

A man, he assessed to be older, perhaps in his seventies, hung by his right leg only, upside down and halfway up the middle rope of the three bell pulls that dangled from the belfry. The man's jacket draped inside out, exposing its purple silk lining. It hung over the head and outstretched arms of the body as they pointed towards the hard chamber floor below. Johnstone imagined a superhero who had frozen in flight, but who still defied gravity.

The man was dead, Johnstone was sure. As sure as he could be. There was no movement in the body itself, and the only sign of breath in the chamber was his. The weight of the body maintained the momentum on the bell and caused it to rotate so that the man's figure moved back and forth and up and down.

On the floor, scattered below the pendulum swing of the body, were several, perhaps a dozen small, wrapped pieces of rock candy. Johnstone bent to examine them more, without touching. Multi-colored on their edge with the words 'WHITBY ROCK' running through them, each word its own arc within their bite-sized tubular form. They looked appetizing and appeared to have spilled from the man's pockets as the rope halted him in his fall. The candy was like that which tourists would buy at seaside towns as a souvenir, but much smaller.

Officer Johnstone scanned around the chamber for any clues to what had happened. It was rare that he would become involved in such a case, and he wondered if he could shed any reason onto the scene. Johnstone made notes as he did so, a detective for a moment. Now, for a minute, he forgot about his breakfast and became Sherlock.

Access to the belfry was via a narrow ladder that did not start at a level that met the floor, but at a height only reached by standing on another object such as a table or chair. There was nothing in place that would enable him, or anyone else, to reach the first rung. So how did the man get up there? At the top of the ladder a small opening, it did not look wide enough to fit someone of the stature of

Johnstone. It was the only way into the belfry, there was no other way up there.

The body continued to swing back and forth, but now with less arc, the sound of the bell reduced in frequency and volume. Johnstone tilted his head to one side and noted that the man looked slimmer than him. Maybe the opening was wide enough to allow the man through with little trouble. The body would need to come down, but he could not do that, not even with help. He would wait for the crime team but would call in a ladder so that they could access the body. And anyway, the forensics team would examine the scene first.

Meanwhile, in Scarborough, forty minutes away by road to the south, Detective Inspector Mary Hunter was returning to her hotel, the Great Eastern, after a morning jog. She would have breakfast, then set about preparing a training update she was delivering to a few police officers later that day in Whitby. Hunter had been with the North Yorkshire Police Force for five years and had risen through the ranks at an impressive rate. They had involved her in several high-profile cases, such was her tenacity and reputation.

Her last case concluded only months ago. A three-year investigation resulted in four men and one woman being convicted of being associated with an organized crime group, whose activities included money laundering through local businesses to foreign bank accounts. It disappointed her that she had not discovered the source of the cash that flowed through their organization.

As she entered the hotel, the clerk at the reception desk called her over and handed her a note. A message from the duty sergeant at Whitby police station, to call back regarding an incident at a local village.

Relieved, her preparation for the training had not even begun. Hunter had weeks to think about the content but, as usual, had left it to the last possible moment to organize the presentation. She knew they would find her out one day, not the star that they thought, a pretender. Not because she was a woman or because of her color, there was another demon lurking within her soul, one that no-one suspected could be there, but one that drove her, the reason for every decision she made and every success she had.

Back at the church, PC Johnstone viewed the scene. Was this a suicide? It did not appear to be a straightforward conclusion. How did the man get up there without help to reach the ladder? Would hanging by a leg be enough to cause death? If not suicide, who did this? And for what reason? It made little sense that all of this had happened in the ten minutes that the Reverend had described. The time that the bell had sounded before the body, an already dead body, found hanging.

Johnstone could not fathom it, there were more questions, but he was too hungry to give it any more consideration. The team would arrive soon, and that was their job. His belly reminded him with a hopeful rumble request for breakfast, that he was not the detective here. The candy was on the floor, all around where he stood, scattered at random. He pushed one piece aside with the toe of his right boot; the steel within its sole scaped along the stone floor. His belly growled again. Surely, no-one would miss just one piece.

3
CLARITY

T here are moments of clarity of mind and deed, there are also, in the majority, moments of organized confusion that fill all in between, never memorized or even recalled as such.

It had been forty-five minutes since officer Johnstone had wandered into the church to find the cause of the ringing bell. Now the bell was silent. Reverend Coombs sat at the entrance to the chapel, still in shock. A small crowd of onlookers greeted the van that carried the crime team as it arrived and parked close behind Johnstone's vehicle.

Three officers got out of the van and led by Detective Hunter, they marched towards the church and the Reverend, still seated at the chapel entrance. She expected this case to be short to resolve, a report of a hanging body, more likely to be a suicide. She was likely to be appointed to be the senior in charge of this case as she had been scheduled to train officers at the Whitby station prior to the call and, by chance, was the ranking officer. However, it was her intension that the two local detectives who accompanied her were going to do most of the investigation. Headquarters would move her to a higher priority case, she hoped.

"Hello, I am Detective Inspector Hunter."

Coombes did not respond.

The Inspector repeated her introduction. The Reverend, sitting and for a moment startled as he realized the vision of three police officers standing in front of him, stood upright with the rapidity of a jack-in-the-box. He fumbled with his fingers, reaching behind his left ear.

"Sorry, my hearing aid. I turned it off because of the bell."

"OK, I am Detective Hunter. Can you tell me what is going on here? And what bell?"

Without warning and as if in answer to the question, the sound of a bell started again from high in the tower. Only it was not the same bell. To those who knew, it was its neighbor and partner in Sunday peals, less than an octave higher. The ringing had not deterred the spirits from returning to the scene. The Reverend looked to the tower open mouthed before he spoke with a quiver in his voice.

"He is in there, your colleague. He is in there. I do not know what is going on. He told me to wait here and has not been back out." Coombs said.

"Thank you, Reverend, we will confirm." Said Detective Hunter.

Now, she had little information regarding the incident. Johnstone had not responded to calls. The last time that control had heard from him was when the PC had requested a ladder or platform some thirty minutes earlier.

"The bell, it has been sounding for a long time?" She said, as she pointed with her gloved hand to the belfry.

"This one, no. It has just started. The other was ringing before." Replied the Reverend.

"The other?"

"Yes, the other bell was ringing first. That is why I came here, I told that to PC Johnstone. This is a different bell, there are three up there."

"Right, we will talk with PC Johnstone. Thank you. Please remain there for a moment."

Before she took a step, she looked around the graveyard and to something close to a large oak tree. Hunter turned back to the Reverend to question him again.

"Why have those three graves been dug out? Over there, under the oak tree."

In the far corner of the graveyard, someone had stacked three neat piles of earth dug from the graves beside three similar looking headstones.

"Oh, my Lord, there are no burials planned, and those are existing graves! They have desecrated them!" said Coombs, now in a state of total shock.

"You come with me." Hunter turned to the closest of the two junior detectives behind her and pointed to the entrance door. Then addressing the other officer, she said.

"Stay here and get statements from the Reverend and the locals." She pointed to the small gathering at the gate of the graveyard.

The two marched into the nave. They could hear the bell and some activity coming from the chamber and headed that way. When they arrived at the bell ringing chamber, a strange composition met them. Under the ladder to the belfry, flat against the stone wall, stacked in a neat vertical triangle of steps, was a pile of books.

On inspection as her eyes focused, she realized they were hymn books, collected from the pews of the nave. Someone had sorted and arranged them with their red spines and embossed gold titles laid in the same direction, and by doing so had created a step sufficient to reach to the ladder. The gilded lettering reflected and added a surreal organized permanence to the structure.

The bell continued to sound, Hunter looked up through the darkness and on its rope was Johnstone. Johnstone was at an equal height to the body. He hung and swayed, his left hand gripped the bell pull, his feet wrapped around the rope. The other hand stretched towards the now still body of the man. He reached into the jacket pocket of the body, just. Hunter called.

"PC Johnstone, what are you doing there?"

"I need to get this…" Said Johnstone, frantic in voice and movement. He grasped further, stretched too far. His grip on the rope failed, his fingers lost their purchase, his other hand grabbed for the jacket but failed, and he fell. Hunter and the officer could only stand and watch. Each emitted a brief gasp as Johnstone tumbled from the rope right in front of them. They could not stop the fall. Two bells rang without companionship, as gravity called.

Now, in a matter of minutes after her arrival, there were two dead men in the bell tower as Johnstone's head hit the cold stone floor before any other part of his body and a sickening crack echoed between the sound of the strikes of the bells. His head took the full force, and, in an instant, he was gone, and so were all but one of the Whitby Rock candies. As his right hand released its grip on life, it also released its hold on the last candy in the church, as it sat, balanced in the center of his palm.

4
RELEASE

Without hesitation, Detective Inspector Hunter pulled up her cuffed jacket sleeve, removed her glove and extended two fingers to check Johnstone's neck for a pulse. The body warmer than her touch but with no sign of life. Hunter turned to Detective Basford, who was standing at her side frozen by more than the cold. He was a tall man in his late twenties, new to his position and unfamiliar with such events. The seconds after the fall stunned him into inaction and he wavered, unbalanced until his feet repositioned to save him from embarrassment.

"Are you OK, Basford?"

"Yes, ma'am."

"Well, we have a bit of a mess here, don't we?"

"Yes, ma'am."

"Now. Go outside and radio for the full forensic team. We will need a ladder and platform so we can get the body down. An ambulance and the fire service."

"Yes, ma'am." Basford said. Lost for words other than to confirm Hunter's orders. He walked as fast as he could to the van to call control for assistance.

Hunter gathered the scene in her mind's eye, creating a three-dimensional picture before following Basford out of the church. The bell slowed and became more discordant. Reverend Coombs raised himself from his crouch and grimaced as he stretched out his legs and his knees cracked. He fumbled behind his ear to turn his hearing aid on again. It emitted a high-pitched whistle as he faced Hunter.

"Reverend."

"Yes."

"We have called for additional help. They will arrive soon. Before they do, can you tell me more about the graves over there? The ones tampered with?"

"Yes. Well, there are no burials planned in that area. So, someone has dug out the earth for some other reason. Not deep by the look of it. Those stones are unidentified. No markings apart from some initials and a year, but all in the same carving and design. There are always new flowers at the center stone, a new arrangement in the vase each week. We do not know where the flowers come from or who brings them here, but they always appear there, always."

It took the forensic team another thirty minutes to arrive after being called. Without need for urgency, the ambulance and fire service got to the scene soon after that and waited for the forensic team to do their work. Hunter watched on as the team photographed and dusted the bell chamber, nave, and doorways. Exhibits collected, described, placed, and numbered into clear plastic bags, sealed, and logged. Johnstone's body photographed and transported without comment or need for lights or siren from the scene by the ambulance. The fire service built a platform in the bell chamber which allowed the team to reach the ladder and to examine the belfry before releasing the body, complete with the entire bell pull rope still wound around its leg.

5
PERCEPTION

A s with any part of reality, our perception of an event is not what another may see. There are different dimensions to each viewpoint. Our own prejudices and personality bias may corrupt distance, time, and space. What you perceive as being in plain sight may be a mere shadow to others. A figment of a happening.

The day after the incident at St. Bridget's, Detective Hunter returned from her training assignment in Whitby with more baggage than she had expected. Besides her travel luggage, there were now a handful of case files and statements that she would need to review. She sat in the first-class carriage on the train from Middlesbrough to Northallerton. There were no direct trains from Whitby, so she had taken a taxi to Middlesbrough station and boarded the Trans-pennine Express. The journey would only take half an hour, just enough time to read through some handwritten statements taken by the officers outside of the church.

She pushed her coffee to one side and set the folder on the table in front of her as the train gathered speed and the landscape streamed by. Hunter stripped off the brown elastic strap that secured the folder, opened it, and read the notes and interviews taken at the scene of the incident at St. Bridget's church. The first from Reverend Coombs.

It was 6 a.m. when I woke, and as I would on most mornings, showered, dressed, and prepared my breakfast. I put the morning news on TV and sat to eat. It was then that I noticed the bell. That is why I went to the church. It should not have sounded; the call to worship would not have been until 8 that morning. The time was about 6:25. I knew that because I was waiting for the 6:30 weather report on the TV. I left the house, ran as fast as I could to the church, and saw that the chapel door was open. There was no one else around. It was about 6:30 then. I entered the nave and then went to the bell chamber where the body was hanging. That is when I called the police. PC Johnstone arrived, and I waited outside. The other police van came after and the bell started again.

The next taken from Jenny Wilson. Jenny was a benefits officer at the local council offices in Whitby, where she had worked for the last seven and a half years. She lived a few houses away and on the same street as the church. Number 19, Church Street.

I was asleep, and the loud sound of a van woke me. It seemed to leave in a hurry. The church bell was ringing too. My alarm had not gone off yet, I set the alarm for 6:15 a.m. so it must have been before that, I am not sure of the exact time. I travel to Scarborough to see my mother; she is in a care home there. I leave at 7:30 in the morning. The church does not sound the bell until later, I think. I am not around by then. When I heard the bell, it made a strange ring, not like normal ringing sound. I went to the church when I saw the police car parked out there. The bell stopped and then started again after the other police van arrived.

A statement by Malcom Powers, a farm laborer. He worked in the fields most days, as a shepherd.

I was out tending to the sheep in the far field; I had been out there since four that morning. We had reported a dog running around and disturbing the animals last week. I had spoken to PC Johnstone about it. So, I was checking to see they were all OK. After that I was riding my bicycle on Sneaton Lane, I left the field to return to my house about ten after six and was cycling down the lane. I could hear the bell ringing at the church and saw headlights approaching. They were coming out of the village, travelling quick and sent me into the hedgerow as they passed. They almost killed me then. There were two or three men in that van. The van was white and had a large ladder on the roof. It must have been going to Whitby because that is where that lane goes to. I stopped at the church when I saw all the commotion.

Hunter stopped reading and looked out of the window as the industrial landscape turned into green embankments, fields, and trees as they smeared against the rushing of the train. Why did the Reverend not hear the bell before six twenty-five? There were at least two others in the village who had a different timeline.

Then she recalled Coombs' hearing aid. He did not have it on all the time. He must have turned it on to hear the weather report on the TV that morning. The bells were already ringing before six twenty-five; she knew now as she took a sip of coffee. The cup held onto a perfect imprint of her dark red lipstick as she returned the cup to the table.

6
FORENSICS

t is necessary to understand that the performance of an autopsy will only reveal an interpretation based only upon on factors of exclusion. Elimination of cause and effect of those forces or circumstances contributing to the death of the subject. Informed by application of testing and analysis, the findings will establish those compounds whose function it is to perform in collusion to deliver the end.

Detective Mary Hunter sat at her desk at Police headquarters in Northallerton, England. She had returned to her office after witnessing the incident in Sneaton Thorpe some three days ago and, as she had expected, the case assigned to her and her team, now named the St. Bridget incident.

Two men were dead, one of them a police officer, both under strange circumstances. Now faced with piecing together what had happened that morning, in the minutes before she had arrived at the scene, she spread the evidence before her. Hunter sifted through the many photographs and reports attached to the case.

She was still waiting on more reports in connection to the unknown man. There had been no noticeable cause of death, the only finding from the evidence was that the time of death was less than an hour before they discovered him hanging from the bell rope. They found no identification on the body. No license, photographs, credit cards or any other documents. A small, sealed plastic evidence bag contained the only item found in the body's clothing, a small gold wedding ring, sewn into a jacket pocket. She had to wait to find if the man's fingerprints would shed any light on who he was, where he came from, and what he did.

Hunter moved to inspect PC Johnstone's field notebook. She opened the book to the last entry, the St. Bridget's incident, written in pencil. The neatness of the notes surprised her:

06:44 March 12th, 1998. St Bridget's Church, Sneaton Thorpe. Attended the scene. Unidentified hanging body.

Interview: Rev. John Coombs says he found the body. It appeared to be dead and hanging at 06.30. He was having breakfast. He said that he had heard a bell ringing at 06.25. He saw no-one in the church when he arrived five minutes later. No vehicles. No other witness. Chapel door is open. The Bell is still ringing.

06:47 The bell chamber. Body of man. Age approx. 70, appears dead, hanging from bell rope by right leg. Candy scattered on the floor. A small puddle of water beneath the center bell pull. No way to reach the body as there is no access to the belfry ladder. No steps or way to reach the belfry ladder, too high off the ground.

06:51 Call dispatch for a ladder or steps. Confirm crime scene unit required. We may need fire service to release body. Securing the scene.

Hunter pulled out a stack of more than a dozen forensic photographs and as she examined them, she halted at one in particular. As with all crime and accident scene photographs, they always reveal the cold, stark, dark nature of death, and this was no exception. She gazed at the image of Johnstone's crumpled body, alone and awkward on the hard paved floor of the bell chamber. The picture captured the area of the rectangular, immovable stone flags surrounding the body.

Hunter turned her attention to read the page of Johnstone's notebook again and read to herself, 'Candy scattered on the floor'. She examined the detail of the frame and then found another photograph of the wider area. Hunter held them, one in each hand, side by side. There was no evidence of any candy on the bell chamber floor, none. But something caught her eye, though. In Johnstone's open right palm sat a single, multi-colored candy.

She rummaged through the stack of evidence collected from the scene and pulled out exhibit bag labelled C2. Noted on the bag, a description that confirmed that it was the content plucked from Johnstone's right hand. She held it close to her desk lamp, the brightness burning into the content. Inside, the single candy, alone and still in its own clear wrapper. She examined it further and noted the WHITBY ROCK lettering. Hunter had seen larger versions of this type of rock candy at seaside locations. It brought back memories of when she was a little girl, visits to beaches, toffee apples and candy floss and being at the seaside with her new parents. She thought back to the time when they had adopted her over twenty-seven years ago.

Her daydream broke, and she returned to her examination. Where were the other candies? She did not recall seeing any and, as she sifted through the images, there were none in any of the photographs. She looked through the evidence again and pulled out another sealed plastic evidence bag, labelled C5. Inside it were at least fifteen empty translucent candy wrappers. They appeared to be the same as the one around the candy that was still intact. The evidence bag noted they took these wrappers from Johnstone's right trouser pocket.

Hunter took a sip of her coffee, now a cold brewed beverage reminiscent of burnt coal. She could not spare the time or effort to make another. She forced another gulp down, leaving a brown halo tidemark circle halfway up the inside of the cup, before she opened the autopsy report that related to Johnstone.

Nothing suspicious about the cause of death; blunt trauma to the head, neck and thorax, a cervical fracture severing the spinal cord. Three of them had witnessed the fall, and she had expected that conclusion. She recalled the erratic behavior exhibited by Johnstone prior to his fall and had a hunch that there must be more reason he was climbing on the bell rope. She read the standard blood report. There were the normal indicators that she expected to see. High cholesterol, high blood sugar, last meal sugar candy, but nothing more. She then studied the standard drug test, no trace of heroin, morphine, cannabis, amphetamine, alcohol, or cocaine. No sign of any other intoxicant or drug that could have explained Johnstone's behavior.

Did Johnstone eat all the candy? He had missed his breakfast, but that was not the reason for his behavior, was it? What had caused Johnstone to build the hymn book steps to the ladder which led to the belfry? He had noted and called for a ladder; he knew they would require one. Was it so he could check or release the man? Was there some other urgent need after that call? She recalled that Johnstone's last words were 'I need to get this', and when he had said them, he was reaching towards the body, or the clothing of the body. Hunter also recalled how frantic he had seemed.

She knew more progress may come from a detailed toxicology report. There must be more to find. There must be.

7
COMPOUNDS

There are many compounds man-made or extracted from nature that when digested and absorbed into the human system distort the consumer's view of the world. A trip of euphoria, excitement, happiness, awe, and energy are possible. Otherwise, a spiral of hallucination, anxiety, paranoia, reality shift, restlessness, and disorientation will greet the participant.

A week after the incident, Hunter had received more reports relative to the St. Bridget's church case. Identification of the body, found hanging by his leg on the bellpull, had yielded no lead. The potential cause of death had also been elusive to pinpoint. The forensic autopsy had shown no trauma to the body apart from the marks made on the leg by the rope and bruising to the upper arm. There was some sign of frothing in the lungs, which could be a sign of drowning. She recalled Johnstone's notes that mentioned a small puddle of water on the chamber floor. Hunter realized Johnstone's uniform must have mopped it up after he fell and rested in the same location. Fingerprint analysis had provided no match with anything on the national database. The age of the man looked to have been in his mid or late 70s.

Hunter held exhibit C1 to the light. A sealed plastic bag contained the gold ring, found in the man's pocket. Set with three single cut diamonds at the top, it must have held some importance. She estimated the ring to be a small size, perhaps a six or a seven. Hunter shuffled through the forensic photographs and found a close-up image of the ring. The picture revealed three hallmarks imprinted along the inside edge of the band. They were clear, a cat's claw with three crowns arranged in a triangle, the characters 'Q8' and also letter 'G' beneath a crown. She would need to review what these meant and logged onto her PC to find out more. A slow internet search eventually confirmed what the hallmarks meant. The ring made in Sweden, in 1943 and in Gothenburg. She noted the finding, a Swedish connection. We will send fingerprints from the body to Sweden.

Hunter moved on to consider what had happened to PC Johnstone. He had no history of any concern over his mental health or of his behavior. He was a reliable police officer, respected for his friendliness in the community. There must be a reason for his strange behavior that morning.

She unsealed the large brown envelope that contained the summary sheet of the detailed toxicology report ordered some days ago using a blood sample from Johnstone's body. The report outlined that small quantities of psilocin, psilocybin, and baeocystin were present in the blood. She did not know what all these compounds were or what they did. More information was available from the forensic laboratory online resource. Hunter had heard of psilocybin, could not place where or for what reason. The report did not mention, but the compounds were important enough to warrant them being noted. She logged in, entered the report identification reference, and waited for the full document to download.

8
DOWNLOAD

D etective Hunter considered many things without connection to the St. Bridget case as the download icon circled in isolation in the center of her screen. She cursed the slow internet connection as the minutes ebbed by. This was painful. Her coffee was now cold. Maybe she should use the opportunity to get herself a hot brew from the break room, even though she did not favor the blend that the vending machine offered.

The break room was a compact room on the opposite side of the building, connected by a narrow corridor the walk was always a solitary one. A microwave, a coffee machine, and two snack vending machines crammed around a small table, an uncomfortable space. The modus operandi when using the facility was to grab whatever you needed and to get back to your desk as soon as possible. Hunter thought they intended this, by design, to increase efficiency. As she entered the room an old colleague, Detective John Scott, was waiting for the microwave to ping its confirmation that his sausage roll was hot enough to eat.

"Hey John." Said Mary in her combined Caribbean and English West Country accent.

"Mary! How are you doing?"

"Ok. How are you? What are you up to these days?"

"Ah, I'm good. Working on another fraud case. Number crunching bank accounts. All I can see when I close my eyes are numbers. What about you?"

Mary rinsed her cup and pushed it under the coffee machine, hesitated as she selected latte and replied.

"The St. Bridget's case, the one where the PC died. Sneaton Thorpe."

"Jeez, yes, that's a strange one. Not unusual for that place though!"

"What do you mean?"

"You know, Sneaton Thorpe. The explosion in ninety-two or ninety-three."

"What explosion?"

"Oh, did you not know?"

"No, I was not here until ninety-four, I was in the West Midlands Investigation team before I came here. I never heard of that incident. So, what happened?"

"Oh yes, so you were. Well, the explosions demolished an entire building. It looked like a version of hell. Smoldering for days it was."

"Did they find what caused it?"

"No, no-one saw a thing. They all said nothing."

"Did any-one get hurt?"

"No, I don't think so. Are you having any luck with the case then?"

"Bits and pieces, here and there, you know how it is."

The microwave stopped and pinged to end the conversation. Scott removed the now steaming roll. Hunter returned to her desk with her coffee, the downloaded file icon highlighted at the bottom of the display; she double clicked to open it. The document lit up and filled her screen with a single page.

TOXICOLOGY REPORT
TEST REFERENCE 002030401
DATE: 16th MARCH 1998
SAMPLE: BLOOD TYPE O
TEST SAMPLE RESULTS:
PSILOCIN–MARKER POSITIVE
PSILOCYBIN–MARKER POSITIVE
BAEOCYSTIN–MARKER POSITIVE
NORBAEOCYSTIN–NEGATIVE
SUMMARY

'The positive markers found in the sample; Psilocin, Psilocybin and Baeocystin and are all psychotropic compounds categorized as class A drugs. These compounds have hallucinogenic properties if ingested.'

'The volume of compounds found would have had a substantial effect on the subject. May lead to distortion of the subject's view of the world and potential feelings of euphoria, excitement, happiness, awe, and energy.'

The coffee at her lips did not taste so bad after all. She took another sip. Hunter relaxed and sat back in her chair.

It creaked as she did so. It was old, tatty, and worn, but there was no chance of a replacement. She had never seen a report that had identified these compounds, so had no baseline to what they were. This could be much more than she had first thought. This case had too many questions still unanswered. Who was the man found hanging on the rope? What was his background? How did Johnstone end up with high levels of hallucinogenic compounds in his system? She picked up exhibit C2, shook the bag and stared at the single piece of 'WHITBY ROCK' candy.

9
BÖRJAN

E ach language has its own colloquialisms hidden in its speech and pronunciation, but when translated the words will always have the same meaning. On Thursday, June 26th, 1941, in Charlottenberg, Sweden, the word början translated as it always did to beginning, as we know now the first thread woven into a complex pattern of history and events.

The town of Charlottenberg sits close to the Swedish border with Norway, an intersection of rail networks connecting the two countries. An area of less than two thousand people had become the focus of supply and demand as the early part of World War II split the two nations apart and on separate tracks. Norway was under German occupation while Sweden struggled to remain neutral.

Edelborg, Ed to his friends, was nineteen, tall with short blond hair. He dressed in unremarkable clothes, a plain jacket, shirt, and shoes that were always clean and polished to ensure he was as inconspicuous as possible. A porter in the town's railway station, nothing more by design, someone who did not warrant attention. That is the way he wanted it.

The station building had stood in the center of town, on Statonsgaten since 1865. Its red brick facades and ochre bands of decoration set it with a stronger presence than its wooden neighbor, a café used by travelers as a point of respite. Hot, strong coffee, pies, and pastries greeted passengers as they waited to depart or rested after arrival. It always felt welcoming and warm, whatever the season.

Today, Ed avoided the movement and marching of many German soldiers back and forth from the carriages. He leaned against the waiting room wall and looked on as the heavy freight transport gathered steam in preparedness to depart from platform one. He noted the B class steam locomotive had replaced its Swedish identification with a Norwegian one. The train driver and his mate stood by as staff from the depot puffed and panted as they shoveled coal from the tender to the boiler furnace, the flames illuminating their sweat laden faces. They had been at it for three hours, re-establishing the slow burn that existed when they had kindled the engine earlier in the day. Now, pressure and heat were building, copper and steel were at a working temperature. The driver and his engineer took control of the cab. Excess steam spilled on to the surface of the platform from the boiler, a gray whirling tide that hid the boots of marching feet from view as the soldiers set to embark.

As he stood, he considered his conversation a moment before with a junior nurse he had met in the adjacent café. She looked to be in her early twenties, her dark hair tied up and hidden under a white cap, a nurse, recognizable, from the small red cross in the center of the hat and above her forehead. The nurse sat alone at a table in the corner, her head bowed, a coffee cupped between her palms. She considered the drink with concentration, a case wound and tied with a string at her feet. Ed suspected that she was German; he knew a mediocre amount of that language, enough to make conversation. It was an opportunity to get information, but it was also important to him to check if she was alright.

"Do you need any help with your case, Miss?" Asked Ed in German. The nurse replied in manageable Swedish.

"Oh. I am from Oslo, I am Norwegian, not German, and the case is not heavy, I can take care of it, thank you. We have to keep it by our side at all times," she said, looking around the café. There were only four others in there, and they were at the other side of the room. Ed knew that most Norwegians could understand and speak Swedish, even if the pronunciation was off. It made him more relaxed, and he felt comfortable talking to her.

"You are not eating. You should take some food with you, here is a pie, I just bought it." Said Ed as he handed her a fish and potato pie wrapped in brown paper.

"Sorry, thank you. But I cannot accept any packages, Engelbrecht has ordered. We both will be in trouble if I accept anything, I do not assume that we will stop before Haparanda. We have sufficient on the train. I hope."

"I wish you a safe journey Miss, my name is Ed."

"Thank you, Ed, I am Reidun. Rei. I do not know if I will be back." She said, her eyes filled with tears. Reflected in them the café windows and the evening sky. Ed knew.

"You do not want to go, do you?"

"No. I am made to."

"I can help?"

"How?"

"You know where the ticket office is?"

"Yes."

"If you want help, go there in five minutes." Said Ed. He would help her get away. The platform guard blew his whistle, calling the troops and medical staff to board the train. They did not have long.

Ed left the café and returned to platform one, walking past the engine and towards the ticket office. From their conversation, he now knew General Engelbrecht was onboard. They knew him well in this area, the commandant of the German 163rd Infantry Division, based in Norway since the invasion. Ed's knowledge of the rail system informed him that the destination, Haparanda, was on the border with Finland. He knew that the route would take the train through Sweden using the track via Laxå, to Hallsberg, Krylbo, Ånge, Vännäs, Boden and then to their destination. Why would they be going there? Why through Sweden, a neutral country?

He did not know the war was going so much in the Germans' favor they were moving towards another plan. Operation Barbarossa was that plan, the invasion of Soviet Russia through Finland. Yes, Sweden was neutral, but to negate German threat had agreed to allow the transport of military personnel and equipment from Norway to Finland on its rail system, something that would weigh on the country for many years after the war.

Ed would report the movement to his contact, an Englishman, now in Stockholm, who he had met when he was seventeen, almost two years ago, when he had helped to unload the man's luggage as he arrived in town. The Englishman used the name Karlsson, Ed knew that this was not his actual name but a disguise to cover for his activities.

He did not favor a foreign power to dictate his country's fate, or the German occupation of Norway. Ed used his job as rail porter to cover for his participation with the Swedish resistance, or the Tuesday Club, as Karlsson called it.

Sheltered by his job, he could report on rail transport movements from and to Charlottenberg, just like today. In addition, he sometimes would help get various items across the border to Norway. Many goods were becoming scarce, sugar, coffee, bread, butter, meat, eggs, and dairy products were all in short supply. The ability to access rail cars and his knowledge of the rail network allowed Ed to develop a competence for moving anything, including people across the border, but all this was dangerous, and he knew one mistake could lead to his seizure and execution.

He continued to walk towards the ticket office. Where was Rei? They were boarding the train. If she did not come, then it would be too late. It was 8 p.m. The sun was low in the cloudless sky but would remain to light the day for another two hours. There, as Ed weaved between soldiers, stood Rei, waiting at the entrance to the ticket office. Ed passed her without looking.

"Follow." Said Ed, relieved. He had taken a risk, but she was there!

He arrived at the south end of the building; Rei followed a few steps behind. Above, a brick inlay on the wall read 'CHARLOTTENBERG'. Underneath and behind a dense screen of landscaping was a doorway. Ed first glanced around. As the troops boarded the train, he pushed apart the shrub enough to make a passageway, Rei followed. Ed unlocked the door, opened it, and they both entered a small room that he used to hide packages, a windowless storeroom.

"Stay here, I have the only key, here lock the door behind me. I will be back when the train has left, and it is dark. You will be secure until I return. Do not answer to anyone else."

Rei flung herself at Ed and wrapped her arms around him. He hugged her tight.

"Thank you." Said Rei.

"Wait until I return." Said Ed.

She looked at him, tears ran down her face in relief.

"We will both get out of here."

10
SMUGGLE

The shadows that accompanied the evening had elongated as far as they could before they had faded with the last rays of sunlight. They left behind them a sky the color of ripened mulberries hewn with the random speckle of distant suns. The cafe now deserted with chairs upturned on tables, the coffee pot cold on the counter, and the pastries already packed away for breakfast. The station was still apart from an unladen freight train waiting to depart to Stockholm on platform two. Sporadic release of steam accompanied by the hiss that followed from various valves and piston seals, the delivery of the manmade clouds the only interruption to the silence.

Ed, with a large duffle bag over his shoulder, rode his bicycle to its normal resting place outside the waiting room at Charlottenberg Station and parked it. He had waited over two hours for darkness and had returned to release Rei from her hiding place, as he had promised earlier. Ed approached the south end of the building and pushed through the dense shrubs with the back of his forearms. He emerged at the storeroom door and knocked. There was no response. He knocked again.

"Rei, it is me, Ed. It is only me; I am alone, you can open the door."

He could hear movement from inside and the rattle of the key as it entered the lock and turned. The door opened. Ed entered, closed the door behind him, and Rei leapt forward and smothered him.

"Oh, thank you, thank you for coming back. It was the longest wait."

"I do as I promise, I always do, and anyway I could not leave you." Ed looked into Rei's eyes and they gazed at each other for a moment that meant more than the time it took.

"What do we do now?" asked Rei, regaining her composure.

"First, let us get you a different coat, and take off your hat."

Ed opened the duffle bag and took out a long, heavy gray coat.

"Here, this will keep you warm and help conceal your uniform."

"Where are we going?" asked Rei.

"There is a train to Stockholm ready to leave in a few minutes. It will only stop for coal and water, there will be no passengers, only us. We will not get there until tomorrow afternoon."

"You will come too?"

"Yes, I said I will never leave you, until you are away from this place. I have a friend in Stockholm, he should be able to help us, I have known him for a while. He is an English guy, yes, he will help. I have food and hot drink here for the journey."

They readied themselves and left the safety of the storeroom. Ed led the way. His three years at the station had taught him where best to cross the platform without notice. He glanced at the train, occupied with fueling the engine the crew did not notice them. He could tell by the ferocity and the regular discharge of considerable volumes of steam that the train was close to departure. He grabbed hold of Rei's hand, looked up and down the length of station into the empty darkness at both ends, and ushered her with a gentle pull across the platforms and tracks and to an empty freight wagon.

They approached the train; no-one had observed them. The wagon door was unlocked and slid open with no effort or sound. Ed helped Rei to climb in by holding her with both hands at her waist and leapt aboard himself. The train jerked as the engine informed the wheels to exert their grip onto the track. He closed the wagon door and then settled with Rei behind some empty wooden crates for the adventure ahead. They would meet with Karlsson in Stockholm, he would help. All they had to do was to keep warm and hidden.

11
CHEMISTRY

O f all the forms of transport available, riding for ten hours on the splintered hard floor of a freight train is not the most comfortable choice. But in times of war, it is perhaps the most reliable. It was late afternoon on June 27th, 1941, on the outskirts of Stockholm in Sweden. Ed looked at Rei as they arrived on the empty freight train from Charlottenberg. She was asleep with her head on his lap. The gentle rocking of the carriage and the silence, only broken by the steady clack of the wheels on the track, was perfect to him.

Ed knew that there was a chemistry between them, and he did not want the journey to end. He looked at the moving pictures of the outside world that appeared through the vertical cracks of the wooden siding of the wagon. Dawn bought the green of the landscape into the carriage, soon interspersed with the grays and browns of the urban area. They moved past houses and industry towards Stockholm Central rail station. The wagon jerked and swayed more, moving side to side as it switched lines and headed into the freight loading area. Rei remained asleep. Ed waited until the train had stuttered and squealed to a stop, then he held Rei's shoulder to rouse her by rocking her back and forth.

"Rei, Rei. We are here. You can wake now."

"We are here now?" Said Rei, as she sat up and rubbed her eyes and threw off the coat that she had been using as a blanket.

"Yes, but we need to wait here and be quiet for ten minutes while the crew disembark. Let us gather all our things together."

They packed up the little that they carried into the rucksack that Ed had brought along. He slid open the wagon door just enough to push his head through. It was clear. He opened it wider before they both jumped out and made their way into the station proper. Ed had contacted Karlsson by telephone before he left Charlottenberg the previous night. They had discussed the situation and would meet in the café on the second floor of the railway station, overlooking the impressive arched atrium. Ed and Rei made their way there and ordered kanelbulle and coffee. Sitting together at a table for the first time since they had met in Charlottenburg, they gazed at each other and chatted, enjoying the rich cinnamon taste of the pastries.

"Do you have family?" Rei asked.

"No, I am alone, my parents are both dead."

"Oh, I am sorry about that, so sorry."

"It happened when I was young, too young to remember them, so I don't think about it. What about you?"

"My family, mother, father, brother and sister are all in Ullevål Hageby, near Oslo. I did not want to leave them, but I did not want to go into the war. I trained at the Ullevål University Hospital; it was close to where we lived. That is how I am a nurse."

"Will you go back there, to Oslo?"

"Not until this war ends. I would like to get my family out, but I know it is too dangerous."

"We should stay together here, what do you think?" Said Ed.

"Yes, I think we shall do that." Rei Smiled.

Karlsson arrived twenty minutes later, Ed and Rei knew they would be together whatever happened next. They stayed in an apartment in the center of Stockholm, that Karlsson arranged. Ed was engaged to work for him and the Tuesday Club. Ed only returned to Charlottenberg once after arriving in Stockholm.

On July 19th, 1941, Ed's detailed knowledge of the rail station in Charlottenberg allowed him to go back there and to plant a bomb, supplied by Karlsson, aboard a German transport train. The train was on its way to Torneå in Finland, carrying ammunition, artillery, fuel, and office supplies to support the German offensive against Russia. The bomb exploded at the station in Krylbo at five o'clock in the morning. It devastated the station. Ed returned to Stockholm afterwards. He often wondered about what would have happened if they had asked him to set the bomb a month earlier, on the troop transport which Rei would have been traveling.

12
TUESDAY

E d took part in many escapades organized by Karlsson and the Tuesday Club from their base in Stockholm, but those are tales for another time. Ed honed his skills and became an expert in smuggling any item on any route, his specialty was the Norwegian border and the rail connections across it. Many people owe their lives to him.

He and Rei stayed together in Stockholm and eighteen months later, in 1943, they exchanged rings; Ed found Rei a gold wedding band set with three diamonds made by a master jeweler on Biblioteksgatan in Stockholm. After the peace came and things returned to normal, they moved to a small house on the outskirts of Gothenburg and settled their married life there.

There was no cause to continue to travel or to smuggle contraband. Ed took a class and ended up becoming a lecturer at Gothenburg Chalmers university. Rei worked in the city hospital, a job they trained her to do based on her previous learning. They moved to Lysekil, north of Gothenburg, just ahead of the birth of their only daughter in 1958. However, a great misfortune befell them. Rei would never meet her daughter as the birth came with severe complications, which she did not survive, as the baby did.

Ed became lost in grief and quit his job at the university, although many still assumed he worked there. He returned to what he knew best, smuggling contraband into and out of Sweden to the Baltic states. His knowledge of chemical engineering allowed him to think and dwell on ideas that would make money, although his resources did not provide enough to implement any of them. Ed's depression led him to lose contact with his daughter, who remained in Lysekil, cared for by Rei's sister, who had moved into the family home from Norway. Ed would send money back home when he had it.

He did not see his daughter again until the morning of May 18th, 1971. One of his business trips returned him to the town. He walked twenty minutes from the docks, past the caviar packing factory and up the hill to Norra Kvarngatan and the school which his thirteen-year-old daughter attended. Ed hid at the corner of Skolgatan, his head peeking around a stone wall as his daughter entered the school that day. He could not bring himself to approach her, she reminded him too much of Rei.

13
FAMILY

On the same day, Tuesday morning, May 18th, 1971, but a sea apart, Mary Brown stood at the window of her room on the second floor of her house on Stanway Road in Birmingham, England. She was nine years old. She gripped and held onto the brown cotton curtain beside her with her left hand; her full attention focused on the street in front.

Many different cars of many different colors took turns to drive past her house without stopping, she was waiting for a blue one. That one would have her new parents. The man and woman that she had seen over the past few months, the ones that would adopt her and take her to a new home. She would try her best to make them like her so she could stay there for a longer time than she had anywhere else.

Here they were, the Hunter's, that would be her new name, Mary Hunter. She liked that name, a powerful name to have. She knew that her new father was a policeman and her new mother worked in an office. Her new home would be with them in another part of Birmingham, she would have a new school and need to make new friends. New was good.

14
BEGINNING

Terrace houses formed the street on both sides, a narrow corridor of red brick and gray slate tile roofs. Inside the small homes, families awaited the return of the day shift from the coal mine. Children released from school were enjoying the few hours of daylight before dinner, then bed.

Today was May 18th, 1971, in Rainworth, a mining village in England and Jack Headland, a small and skinny seven-year-old, had little of importance to take his thought. Jack sat on his favorite branch in an apple tree in his backyard, swinging his legs. The tree had always been there. And whether by design or accident, the branch had grown horizontally from the trunk to form a seat at a perfect height for a small boy.

From his vantage point he could see the railway line, which ran along the boundary of the fenced long rear yard. On occasion, slow-moving rumbling coal trains would pass. Jack would wave at the drivers and they would wave back if they saw him.

Sometimes, if the trees allowed, he could see the pit headstocks and their giant wheels winding up the cages from half-a-mile underground. The branches and leaves made way today, and he could get a glimpse of the machinery. With purpose, the massive iron spoked wheels were rotating, winding. The thick steel cables attached to the cage that contained the men were taut and stressed.

The horn from the mine sounded to signal the end of the day shift and the start of the next. But today it sounded three times rather than the usual one, haunting and lingering like the call of the blue whale. Jack offered no mind to it and continued to sit in the tree. He knew his father would return and it would soon be time for dinner.

After twenty-minutes, Jack's father Arthur pushed through the small wrought-iron gate at the front of the house and walked to the door at its side. You could see from his broad shoulders and gait that Arthur was a coal miner. All his family were coal miners, his father, grandfather, and uncles. It was all that he had, all that he had known. He opened the door to the house and the kitchen; he hesitated and called out to Jack. Jack, now hanging by outstretched arms from the apple tree, fell into a heap on the ground.

"Jack! Jack, come here!" Said Arthur. An urgency expressed in the forcefulness of his voice.

Jack recovered from his heap and stood upright, brushed himself down to release the grass and leaves that had collected on his clothes. He knew from experience, the only time that his father called to speak to him before dinner was to punish him for something. There was nothing he could think of that he had done wrong. With apprehension, Jack sauntered up the garden path to the house to the kitchen door. He entered with no hurry; Arthur broke the silence.

"Jack! In here!" Said Arthur, calling from the dining room.

Jack walked through the kitchen; he passed his mother, who was at the sink and motionless. The smell of boiling vegetables and meat roasting meant dinner was close. He was hungry and hoped that he would have the opportunity to enjoy the meal. The comforting sound of bubbling and sizzling remained in his ears as he made his way from the kitchen into the dining room.

At the table, the figure, slumped and broken, was not what Jack had expected, this was not his dad. He approached closer, walking through the sun as it came through the curtains and illuminated coal dust released into the air from his father's clothing. He was confused. His dad always showered at the mine before returning home, but today he was filthy from his ten hours underground. Jack moved to look at his father's face and saw it for the first time. Pale tracks washed into the coal-stained skin meandered down from Arthur's eyes, avoiding the unshaven bristles, to his jaw. Jack knew then that the world he had known and expected had shifted. His father was a man who did not show emotion and was someone who did not cry, but today he had.

"Yes, sir?" Jack said with some hesitation. He feared the worst.

"Sit down, son."

"I want to talk to you."

"You are not in trouble."

Jack felt the tension in his body resolve and his shoulders relaxed their hunch.

His father continued.

"I know you are doing well at school."

"That is something that you should be proud of. I am."

"I never got the chance to think I had a choice. Nobody told me. Not my dad, not my grandad, nobody."

"You, Jack, you have a choice."

"You can make a choice to do well at school and get a good job, or you can go down the mine."

"Arthur hesitated and struggled to hold back tears."

"Jack, after what I have seen today, people got hurt. My friends got badly hurt."

Jack recalled hearing the three horn blasts. It must have meant something had gone wrong.

Arthur looked into Jack's eyes and said with purpose.

"I do not want to see any son of mine down that pit and observe what I have just seen. Not without knowing the choice."

"The thing is you can choose Jack. You can get out of this place if you want to. Try to do your best at school, it is up to you, no-one else. That is the last I will say on the matter."

"Now, go away and think about that choice. It is your choice."

It was not unit a few years later that Jack learned of what had happened that day; a collapse of a coal seam had killed several miners, his father's workmates, and friends. He knew at that moment that the conversation he had with his father that day when he was seven years old was the start.

15
START

I t was raining this morning, Tuesday the 17th of March 1992. A spring day, a day of some importance, of some relevance to the web of destiny, it was the start, but the day was not yet named such.

The damp air had replaced the blue sky and crisp breeze of yesterday, and a gray overcast sheen of low cloud made the sky. A light but persistent drizzle poured onto the street outside the municipal building and soaked all who walked in it.

From the street, close to the town center, the impressive monument that was the council building stood proud. They had cleaned the renovated sandstone façade in the last month and it was now free of grime and soot. Unlike the office buildings to either side, which stood as guards to the historic market town and its mining industry and had the grime to show for it. Inside, at the front of the building on the second floor, a twenty-seven-year-old Jack stood beside his elevated drawing board and close to the window. From the street the black glazing masked any direct view of the interior of the building, unreflective and dark, however, Jack's face was visible as a white oval, appearing as a washed pebble found by chance in a coal pile.

Jack gazed down from his vantage point into the world outside, a view of the street, the main entrance to the building and of the access way where vehicles would pass to the rear parking area. A rush hour full of wet, hunched, and bedraggled pedestrians hurried by on their way to work. What jobs did they do? Where did they work? Why? Did they look forward to each day? He thought, but not for long and without projection of their lives, as there was no need. He was learning to set aside matters outside of his control.

Jack had left school almost ten years earlier, determined that he would not go down the coal mine. With scant opportunity available, he had worked by helping people he knew in the village, in activities that were not within the law. The wild west of the coal mining area, that was the nature of the village he grew up in, He stayed out of trouble and, through a piece of luck, had found work in the town planning office. Jack had not wasted the years prior to that, he had learned about things that many would never experience. This job gave Jack the ability to do what he loved, planning, sketching, and designing. He did not need to wonder of other lives and their day-to-day complications. It was the first proper job Jack had and to him and his past circumstances, this work was the best and he looked forward to starting each day.

Taped on his drawing board, a landscape plan, it was almost complete. The meticulous detail brought a hint of color to the office, albeit limited to various shades of green. Jack viewed the plan and propped himself by his elbows on the board to consider the last touches to his masterpiece. As he did, he drifted into a subconscious muse, as was his wont, to somewhere not yet arrived.

In this place, a distant voice, like the sounding of a rumbling volcano, disturbed Jack. It was Jeff; he was Jack's manager and in charge of the department. Jeff, a middle-aged child of the fifties, had experienced the heady days of the late sixties as a teenager. Living in a commune and squatting in various locations.

Jeff's interest in town planning born from his sense of social injustice that middle class folks carried with them like packs on a mule. In effect he was still there, in the sixties, frustrated with society and the bounds it fed off. His desire for equality and equity caged. He was not a communist, but someone who saw that everyone should have equal opportunity to earn their way. Jeff was a closet capitalist whose appearance curated by combining the likenesses of a compendium of South American dictators. A mop of hair and an unkempt beard disguised his angular features, which many had remarked could have seen him as an extra on any popular science fiction set. A tweed jacket styled with dark brown leather elbow patches, worn over bright mustard-colored trousers, completed his wardrobe. Jeff stood beside his desk in the office's corner and shouted his questions towards Jack with the melody of a strangled grizzly bear. His beard rustled onto his brown cotton shirt collar as he did so.

"How many Oak trees Jack?"

"Twenty-three Quercus Rubra, yes, we have twenty-three trees specified here." Jack said, answering without hesitation, using the Latin name for the species of oak trees for greater calming effect.

"Thanks, that sounds like plenty to keep the neighbors happy, annoying Nimbies. Will the trees be available for planting to our schedule? Will you have plan finished today?"

"Yes, I checked with the tree nursery. They have all the plant material in stock. A couple of hours and I should have this complete. I spoke to all the neighbors and they are all OK." Said Jack as he continued to draw, keeping his head down and avoiding eye contact.

"If it does the job that we need it to, there's no need to spend much more time on it. Let me know when you finish. We need to get those plans out to the landscapers today so they can order the trees. That reminds me just time for me to order some glass for my greenhouse, I broke a whole side of it at the weekend." Said Jeff, as he returned to sit at his cluttered desk. Fingers shuffled through unorganized piles of paper until he found and pulled out a scrap of paper carrying a scribbled phone number. He squinted to read the note and picked up his desk phone before punching the buttons as though he was sending an SOS Morse code message.

"Yes, hello. I need to place an order for some single pane sheets."

"Can you cut to size? Good and you can deliver?"

"Only to town?"

"Right then, the sizes I need. Ready?"

"Oh. My name, it is Jeff Millstone. Yes, Millstone. That is M. I. Double L. Stone."

"So, I need seven at eighteen by twenty-four. Yes, that is in inches."

"Well, I'm sure that you can convert."

"Ten at twenty-four by twenty, yes."

"And six at twenty-two by twenty-six."

"Yes, twenty sheets, yes."

"What is the cost?"

"Sounds good. You can deliver at the rear of the Council Office on Nottingham Road. I can pay with cash."

"OK, about four-thirty."

"Great, see you then." Said Jeff as he replaced the scrap of paper into its appropriate pile on his desk. He stood, maybe too quick, almost losing his balance, and hurried to stand beside Jack at his drawing board. Jeff, now motionless, stared at the almost completed landscape plan. Jack heard Jeff breathing over his shoulder and waited, in an awkward moment, for the conversation to begin.

"This looks good. You did a good job with this. A wonderful job." Said Jeff, murmuring.

"Thanks." Said Jack, underestimating the important statement.

"I realized you have been with us for a couple of years now. We need to get you moving along. So, I would like to talk about getting you on some training, it will help with your career progression here." Said Jeff as he continued with greater clarity.

"The Council will pay for the course; it is in the budget. Your commitment is to stay with us for a period after you qualify. After that, go wherever you want to. It is your choice of specialty. Engineering, architecture, or town planning. I will leave it to you. Let me know in the next week and I will get the paperwork done."

"Will do, fantastic, just what I was hoping for, thanks Jeff." Said Jack. He sat moving upright in his chair before slumping back over his drawing and rubbing his back. Jeff walked back to his desk.

Taken aback, Jack stared, without blinking, out of the window, and watched the pedestrians scurry by. He smiled to himself. Pleased that his career was progressing, he knew he had created a choice through his own efforts.

16
PHOBIA

I t felt like mid-afternoon, because that is what it was, a warm, blustery fall day. Although it was a day without a page. Jack was here with anticipation of achievement, something that was in his control. Wherever here was. He walked on with a group of friends, but they were unfamiliar friends. He knew them, yet he did not know them. There was no comprehension of why he was there, that was part of the discovery. Unconcerned; he wandered on and followed a compacted gravel pathway that corralled the group, shoulder to shoulder, towards their destination with no discussion or speculation.

Highlighted by the low sun, and viewed through branches and landscaping, stood a tall, impressive twelfth century stone building. It was still a distance away. Jack somehow knew it was a university of renown, an establishment that had history and prestige. His feet now directed to follow a paved path that straightened like an arrow to its target through equidistant maple trees on both sides of the path. A canopy of yellow and gold fall leaf held onto the branches with their last grip and formed a physical marker to the route. He noticed, in the far corner of his eye, in the closest tree a red bicycle that dangled by its frame from a branch; it was high. A bicycle in a tree? It was odd, but he did he not think any more of it.

Jack continued on his journey, now the others were not there, he was alone. After a time, disproportionate to the distance traveled, being shorter than it should, he grew closer to the building. The upright guard of trees and their canopy parted, and now a view of the frontage of the building became close. Shadows on the impressive façade of hand carved detail and delicate decoration, made greater in contrast by the low sunlight.

The light played and danced across arched window openings, pilasters, and columns. A tall and broad opening that had no other purpose than being the entranceway positioned itself at the center of the building. Its sides supported heavy wooden doors of remarkable height and thickness, they opened inwards to the hall.

Above the entrance hung a banner sign, a taught material of red background and white lettering. The typeface of the poster designed as a contemporary and simple message. A vision pointing the subconscious mission towards the university, a place for new understanding and learning.

'CITY UNIVERSITY ENROLLMENT.'

'BUILD YOUR FUTURE.'

Jack felt a comforting spirit within him, he was in the perfect place to start towards a new chapter, to make his choice. He continued through the main entrance into the City University hall. Once inside the building, it was as though he had stepped into another world. The hall, a vast open space, only confined at its extent by a high buttressed ceiling. Tall windows allowed defined sunbeams to illuminate dust particles that hung in the air. Technology overwrote all traces of the historic exterior building design with high-tech displays, desks, and cubicles. This was a polished area, manicured to present the future. The University logo, a silhouette of a bird in flight within a roundel, hung on the far wall. Smaller signs and pennants at various locations within the hall read:

'CITY UNIVERSITY.'

'Enroll now to TRANSFORM your DESTINY and BUILD the WORLD.'

'SCHOOL OF ENGINEERING, ARCHITECTURE AND TOWN PLANNING.'

With no recall of any passage of time, Jack found himself at the enrolment desk. He heard a familiar voice, somewhere in the distance, across the hall, growing closer. The voice called his name.

"Jack!"

"Jack!"

"For heaven's sake, Jack!"

The words brought Jack to the present; he woke with a jump from his daydream. His fantasy world broken. He glanced to the office clock, two fifteen. Two fifteen? Where was he? Back at his desk! Jeff stood beside him, perturbed. It frustrated him that Jack had not yet completed the drawing. He expected it to be ready, it should have been.

"Yes, sorry yes, hmm, Er just concentrating on this." Said Jack, as he shuffled to reacquaintance himself with the present.

"So, are you done then?" Said Jeff.

"Yes, well, almost done. Just need to get some copies run so we can send out. I need to go down to reprographics. I will get four, yeah?"

"Yes, four will do. When you have done that, come out to the car park and help me load the glass delivery. It is here. They came early and dumped it right outside, I do not want it to get damaged."

"OK." Said Jack as he nodded in agreement. He raised himself from his chair and removed the tape that secured the plan at each of its corners to the drawing board. The back of his hand brushed off the drawing before he rolled it up, not too tight, and headed out of the office towards the elevator.

In most circumstances he would take the stairs, as he did not trust the elevator since it failed last month and trapped two members of staff within its walls. That was a story, held and disclosed to grandchildren around a blazing campfire. He recalled it in his mind; it was easy to remember, he ran through it again.

The day it happened the office was quiet, everything was normal. Just after lunch, two people entered the elevator together. They were Helen, a senior administrative assistant. She suffered from claustrophobia. Helen had sought help for her affliction, and her psychotherapy sessions had convinced her to push the confines of her fear. She did just that when she pushed button number two to close the elevator door and was proud of herself for doing so.

The other individual involved, by pure coincidence, was the only agoraphobic in the building. Poor George, a building inspector whose agoraphobia was not a fear of open spaces but a fear of not being able to escape from stressful situations. The confines that he would face in a moment would place him on a cliff edge of emotion.

Helen and George would meet their worst nightmares in the elevator when it lost power and halted between floors. The elevator stopped, the lights dimmed, and the emergency system lit up. They broke the sudden silence within a matter of seconds. The atmosphere of the office changed, and hair stood on end throughout the building. The occupants of the elevator did not waste any time. They replaced the frantic calling of the emergency buzzer with a guttural howl that started deep within the belly, then increased in octave through the throat until the pitch was inaudible to human ear. The chorus of primeval screams of the two permeated every space throughout the workplace, like the bitter smell of burned microwaved popcorn. The disturbance lasted for a good two hours before the elevator became operational and surrendered its captors.

They were both carried sobbing and shaking from the building by a team of rescuers. Neither had yet returned to their work.

Now, in his head, Jack could still hear them. It was no effort to do so; the event burned into the memory of many. The daydream episode had cleared, but he remained unsteady on his feet. He had been out of it for a good while, so the elevator it was. The very moment that Jack pushed the call button, the elevator doors opened. It was meant to be. He stepped inside, half expecting the walls to exhibit evidence of the finger scratching, kicking, and biting that the screams had described. There was nothing. He felt better now. The elevator descended to the ground floor and jerked to a halt. After a moment, the doors opened, and Jack stepped out. No screaming required today, he remarked to himself.

17
COPY

Reprographics, this was the place where you could get anything copied or printed, singular or in bulk. The process held in this room would turn reams of pristine bleached paper into reports, leaflets, posters, brochures, letters, plans or any other printed form. It was the heartbeat of the bureaucracy, where politics and policy formed a perfect partnership. The process did not care of the content or of its accuracy, only that the machines reproduced the copy as commanded. Feeding documents of all shapes and sizes through photocopier machines at tremendous speeds before spitting out their clones. The output from the copiers arranged in neat and ordered piles, collated, and stapled as required, and then carried off for utilization. The amount of paper that the machines consumed was beyond imagination, fifty copies a minute by each machine. A solitary person administered all this industry, she was precise, reliable, and consistent. Jack admired her.

Emptied, the elevator closed its jaws behind him to seek its next victims. Jack turned right and headed to the reprographics room. He pushed open the heavy soundproofed door and entered the space. The lighting illuminated the room far brighter than any other room in the building. The light hit his eyes and caused him to squint, it always did, but he could not help it. A churning clack, clump, click, metallic wall of sound met him. It was hard to hear, never mind make sense of anything. Four heavy duty copier machines functioning at maximum speed, each creating an asynchronous rhythm with the others. Produced to order, an endless death rattle accompanied the paper copies as they ejected from the machines into the end stops of their respective trays. He looked around at the copiers, his senses adjusted and became accustomed to the cacophony. Disappointed, he noticed the large size print machine was also in use. His job, the full-sized plan, needed that machine to get his work out on time. He needed to get ahead in the queue, and he needed to do it now.

In the far corner of the reprographics room, sat a blond-haired petite female figure almost hidden between piles of print materials and finished jobs. It was Angie; she was busy reading; she was the operator and controller of all the jobs scheduled for print. Today there were many, too many for Angie to complete before she left work.

"Hey, Angie." Said Jack, waving at the same time.

Angie did not respond.

Jack approached closer to Angie. He had known her since he had started his position with the planning department. He found her attractive but had never got the nerve to ask her out. Maybe there would be an opportunity now? As he broke into her view, Angie looked up and waved.

Jack in a moment and without hesitation formed his right hand with the fingers flat together and thumb crossing his palm. He raised his hand, in the same configuration, to the side of his head and made a half salute while saying hello and smiling. Angie responded in the same manner. Angie is deaf. Jack had learned some basic sign language hoping to connect with her. At first, he thought, to better communicate, but soon thereafter he realized it was because he liked her. He liked her, he admitted it to himself. The conversation between them became a mixture of sign language and lip reading.

"Noisy!" Said Jack signing.

"Does not matter to me!" Angie responded with a sign and a grin. Jack felt better when Angie smiled.

"Yeah, Horses? Today?"

Jack looked over Angie's shoulder and pointed at the newspaper as she played with her hair between her fingers.

"Yes, I need some winners." Said Angie as she refocused her attention.

I think I can help. Jack signed and smiled again. He picked up a pen and looked through the race card. He understood numbers and had always been interested in trying to figure out patterns, systems, odds and the correlation between different factors and results, from football to horse racing.

Jack had been studying handicap races and the factors that gave a better chance of finding the winning horse. He looked at the race information. His picks would need to come from races that weighted according to the distance run. In which only twelve horses were competing, where the handicap was at a mid-point of the field. And where the candidate horse had placed in a particular sequence in the past three races. Using these factors and applying his own weighting between them, he could point to horses that had a good chance of winning. The odds for each needed to be three to one or better.

As he considered each race, he picked up a pen and circled horses that met his criteria and calculated algorithm.

He started highlighting horses, all running on the 17th, March 1992. All weather tracks at Fontwell, Leopardstown, Nottingham and Southwell.

2:30 In the Spotlight, 4:30 Mic-Mac Express, 2:50 Lanigans Wine, 4:50 Old Talka River, 2:45 Premier Princess, 3:45 No Escort, 5:15 Strath Royal, 7.30 Abergele and 8.00 Inswinger 8/1.

Jack picked up Angie's calculator and entered all the odds. He scribbled on the newspaper. You get over 10 million to one if all these wins! He put the pen back from where he found it.

"Easy picks." He signed with a shrug.

"You sure? You bet also?" Asked Angie.

"Yes, I am sure. And No, these will only work for you. My choices do not win for me, but it is your choice." Said Jack. He smiled again.

"Now, what can I do for you?" Said Angie as she folded the newspaper and stood. Jack thought now may be a good time to raise his interest.

"Maybe a meal at the weekend?" Said Jack, flirting and blushing because he had a wish that Angie would see that he liked her and not dash his hope.

"Dream on." Said Angie, signing as she dismissed the comment.

Jack hesitated as he searched his memory for what Angie had signed. She had held the index finger of her right hand against her forehead before she moved her hand upward and outward, flexing and straightening her finger twice. He remembered, dream, yes, dream.

"In my dream you say yes." Said Jack. Using his recalled knowledge and ability to think fast in reply.

"I only talk work here. Nothing personal, Jack."

"And here is me learning all this sign."

"It gets me to do your work quick through, doesn't it?"

"It is like that, is it? Four copies please of this please, full color, today." Said Jack. He flapped the rolled drawing under Angie's nose.

"You mean in the next hour, then! OK, but these horses better win!" Angie said, pushing the drawing away before grabbing it and depositing it on top of the 'work to do' pile.

"Well, you better start now then. First race is at two thirty." I will see you later.

"See you later." Angie smiled again.

"Not giving up, you know, you are smiling!"

Angie's smile reassured Jack. He was always looking to figure out if Angie had any feelings for him. His mood turned to be more serious the moment that he remembered he needed to meet Jeff in the car parking area outside. That was always an experience.

18
GLASS

We know the frailty of this translucent, transparent, and amorphous solid created from molten sand, ash, and limestone. It can form a fragile material it can break without effort, but such is its structure, we can mold it into a slab powerful enough to stop a bullet. But if it does shatter, entropy determines the shape and destiny of its parts.

Jack had dropped the drawing off into the willing hands of Angie in reprographics. He hurried through the ground floor of the municipal building and into the car park area at its rear. Jeff would be waiting, what could go wrong he thought. Then he recalled many other occasions where events had not worked out the way Jeff had planned them.

No time to dwell, Jeff was already there, standing beside the small, stacked pile of cut-glass sheets he had ordered earlier. Each sheet separated from its neighbor with a layer of cardboard. Jeff needed the glass to replace the several panes he had broken when he had practiced his golf swing inside his greenhouse. The third swing of his four iron had contacted with a twine attached to a zucchini plant. The resultant tangle had carried the complete half-ripened vegetable clean through the end glazed wall of his greenhouse. It took out the twenty sheets of glass which it comprised and ended in the neighbor's garden, complete with the golf club.

The glaziers had delivered the glass when Jeff was busy in a meeting. They had stacked the glass in a location at the end of a planted, landscaped island. It was a location that left the pile exposed to being damaged. That is what could go wrong, Jack confirmed to himself as he assessed the situation as he left the building.

Jeff called to Jack as he approached.

"Hey Jack, they just dumped it here, wait here while I get my car, will you?"

Jeff lurched into a half run, half skip and headed towards his car. A 1986 Volvo 740 estate finished in a dull muddy light brown color. It was only a few steps away from where the glass was located. It is important to note is the fact that this model of vehicle had a long flat roof, perfect for stacking materials. As he reached the car, Jeff felt in various pockets for the keys. Not finding them, he threw both hands into the air.

"Crap, my keys are on my desk!" Said Jeff in exasperation as he looked to the sky.

"Look, help me get this onto the roof. He pointed to the stack of glass. I can get the keys from my office after we have moved it."

Taken aback, Jack was not at all surprised and asked. "The roof? You sure?"

"Perfect, it will be out of the way. Look, it is nice and flat. No-one is going to break it there." Jeff said, convinced that his plan would keep his glass in one piece.

"You sure?" Jack asked again for confirmation.

"Yes, come on, get this sorted."

Jeff and Jack each took turns lifting a sheet of glass from the stack. After some careful maneuvering back and forth from Jeff's car, they balanced the glass on the flat roof. It seemed to be a perfect location. The glass was stable. At that, they both headed back into the office building.

"I have to leave early today, so once I get my keys I will be out of here." Said Jeff.

"No problem, the plans will be ready to go out this afternoon."

"Well done, thank you."

Jack glanced over his shoulder as they entered the building and could not help but shake his head at the sight of the glass balanced on the roof of Jeff's car.

Jack returned to his desk to set up for his next job. He was meticulous in his preparation and always liked to leave his desk and work set up for the next morning. His next project would be to work on a layout for a large reclamation scheme. Something that would differ from anything else the department had ever worked on. It would be very prestigious. A large sewage treatment plant on the edge of town was being decommissioned, and the land turned into an indoor/outdoor sports center. The town had nothing like it. It would be a grand project.

"See you tomorrow, got to go, I am late." Jeff called over to Jack, interrupting his routine.

"Have a good evening." Jack replied, not conscious of his response.

Jack returned to his task and continued to think about the project and the equipment that he would require. Not for long. A familiar voice interrupted his concentration.

"Hey Jack, we're off to the pub tonight to watch the game, are you coming?" Said Neil, the youngest member of the planning team, he conversed as he approached. Neil was just eighteen and straight out of school. He was the office junior and spent most evenings out on the town. His appearance and demeanor most mornings proved this assumption. However, Jack had already figured out what he wanted to do this evening. He wanted to have a quiet time, watch the game on TV with a beer and have an early night.

"I thought, well, I thought they'll crowd the pub out tonight. Everyone will be out because of this game, so I'm just going to watch it at home with a cold beer, nice and quiet." Said Jack in reply.

"But everyone will be there, it will be mega, you know it'll empty the streets. Come-on it's the play-offs. We need you there. Hey. Maybe you could ask Angie?"

"I do not think that would be the best place for her. I do not think she is interested in the game, anyway." Jack unconvinced; he was not sure if Angie felt the same way about him as he did her.

"Angie? You must be blind because that is not what I and others have seen. She likes you." Said Neil in encouragement, knowing that there was something yet to be between Jack and Angie.

A loud crash interrupted their conversation. It came from outside of the building, the sound of sliding, shattering, breaking glass. Jack sat up to peer out of the office window onto the street below.

"Look at that, he's at it again." Jack said and shook his head.

"I knew something would happen; I knew it."

Both Jack and Neil moved closer to the window to get a better view and looked out, not quite expecting to see what they did. Beside his car stood Jeff, his arms gesticulating wildly. Ahead of the car, on the road, laid fragments, and shards of various sizes of glass. He was in such a hurry he had forgotten about the sheets and driven away with them on his roof. As he had stopped the car at the roadway exit, the momentum of the glass had carried it forward, throwing it clear of the car. Passersby and other vehicles stopped at the scene. Nobody had seen anything like it, ever.

"How is he going to get all that cleared up? And look, not a scratch on his car!" Said Jack to Neil.

"He is a nutter, that guy. A real nutter. What about later though?" Neil said, returning to the subject of the previous conversation.

"Well, I know. I just want to watch the game, quiet like. That is all I am looking to do tonight."

"Alright, you know where we will be, yeah? Nag's Head? They have got a great screen. I will save you a seat or two, just in case." Said Neil, hoping Jack would join him.

"Yeah, I might join you later, after they have cleared mess up outside, and I have got to get home to feed the dog, anyway."

"OK, I might see you later." Neil said as he waved to Jack on his way out.

Jack returned to his drawing board and gathered and pack his desk equipment away. He was precise and meticulous in storing all the Rotring drawing pens in their holders and ensuring that their mechanisms were free and working. There was nothing worse than finding that you had to disassemble your 0.25 mm pen into its component parts and clean them all, before you could start your work. The process was messy, and the pen would never be the same when reassembled. He paused, looked through the window and at the commotion outside to assess the situation. A road crew were working to clear the glass and Jeff was reversing his car back into the parking area:

"I will take the back way out today then." Said Jack to himself.

He completed his equipment and desk set up for tomorrow, Jack lowered himself to reach under the desk and pulled out a blue and white motorcycle helmet. He picked up his jacket and left the office.

As he did so, Jeff stormed into the office and towards his desk. He rifled through his desktop and pulled out the scrap of paper containing the phone number for the glaziers. Jeff pushed the number into his phone again and spoke at the moment that it connected him.

"Yes, hello it is me again."

"Millstone. That is M. I. Double L. Stone, Jeff."

"I broke the bloody lot, yes, the lot."

"All of it." Said Jeff, shouting.

"I'm not shouting!"

"Ok, sorry,"

"I just need the order again. Yes, the one in inches."

Jack left his desk and the ongoing telephone exchange. He would use the stairs this time.

19
CALL

The day had started overcast, but by five in the afternoon it had transformed itself into a clear spring evening. Trees had the beginnings of new foliage which glowed a vivid green as the setting sun caught the young leaves in its rays. It was still cold, but even so the sun could deliver a welcome degree or so of its warmth as it approached the horizon.

Jack strode out of the municipal building and into the car park. He needed to get out of the office for some quiet time, away from Jeff and his drama. He was looking forward to watching the game with a beer and whatever he had leftover in the fridge. Maybe the lamb rogan josh takeout curry he had last night. Yes, that sounded like it would go together well with the game.

At the far end of the car park and standing by itself was his motorcycle, a blue and white, 1990 Suzuki GSXR750. The color scheme matched his helmet he had designed himself. He had bought the bike about six months ago and decided that he would ride it at any opportunity, even in the drizzle. Jack glanced back at the office to check if Neil was there. He wanted to avoid him and more questions about watching the game at the pub.

Angie walked out of the rear of the building into the car park and towards her car. A yellow Nissan Sunny. It was her first car, her pride and joy, parked at the very back of the parking area. She chose this spot as it was the least busy and therefore least likely to be the subject of accidental damage by other vehicles coming and going during the day. Angie noticed Jack at the same moment that he looked around; she wanted to catch his eye. That they were some distance apart did not matter. Angie jumped, waved, and signed. He would not miss that, and he did not.

"First two won! Seventy-Five quid!"

"What did I say?" Said Jack, signing back.

"Thank you. You can choose more tomorrow!"

"Maybe you can buy me a drink tonight?" Said Jack in response. He added a heart symbol by forming his hands and fingers into an arrangement that Angie would understand. He was becoming braver with the attempts to get her to come out.

"They have not won yet. Anyway, I am saving for my boat, so dream on." Said Angie as she smiled and signed as she thought about her dream boat, a boat large enough to get to Europe and maybe beyond. That was her ambition to travel solo anywhere in the world. A big boat seemed to be the best way of achieving that, if she could save enough money.

"I will, later." Said Jack as he motioned with a wink and a wave goodbye. They both turned towards their vehicles at the same moment.

Angie got into her car and drove away. Jack looked on as he wiped the still wet seat of his motorbike and started the engine. The bike growled and yelped like a caged animal, an animal glad to see him, he was glad to see it. The clearance from the glass spillage was still ongoing and a line of cars, including Angie's, waited at the exit. Jack got onto his motorbike and weaved between the stationary cars and turned to exit out of town the long way. He did not mind; he enjoyed riding, and the long way would take him out into the countryside and out of the rush hour traffic.

Jack lived in an end terrace house in the same village that he had grown up in. A brick-built house that had been home for many working families before he had moved in. Now the local mine had reduced its capacity, many of the workers had moved elsewhere, and the character of the village was changing. As he arrived home, Jack rode into his driveway and parked his motorcycle in its usual spot near the front door.

As he entered the house, his dog barked then greeted him, jumping as though Jack had been away for a year, the same greeting he had every night.

"Hey, Snoop, how have you been, boy?"

Snoop was Jack's dog, Snoopy. He had been with Jack for the whole of his life, the nine years since he was a pup. Jack had chosen his name from a cartoon strip he used to read and the fact that Snoopy was a cross between a beagle and another breed of unknown origin. He had the long ears of a Beagle, but nothing more than that from that set of genes. The remaining DNA had given him a short brown-

Whitby Rock | Kev Freeman

haired coat and a pointed nose. These together with the ears both confirmed the fact that Snoopy was a mutt.

"Steady on boy, let us get you fed." Said Jack as he pulled a can of dog food from the cupboard and dumped it into Snoops bowl. It reminded Jack of a tasteless school shepherd's pie he was served as a schoolboy, but Snoop loved it.

"There you go, good boy."

Jack felt relaxed. He was looking forward to sitting down with his reheated curry and a beer, no effort required. The ping of the microwave got Jack's attention, and he headed into the lounge with a cold beer and his meal. Jack's lounge decorated only with a couch, a chair, a coffee table, a phone, a TV, and media center. A small red and brown striped rug, there to benefit Snoop, provided the only dash of color.

"Should be kick-off in a moment, boy." Said Jack as he petted Snoop and settled down in front of the TV to enjoy the game.

On cue, the phone on the coffee table rang. He did not have caller identification, so he would have to answer it just in case it was an emergency. Jack pushed the plate of food onto the coffee table. Snoop was interested.

"Shit, every time, every time!"

Said Jack. He answered in a calm voice, disguising his frustration with being disturbed. He soon figured out who it was.

"Hello?"

"You know it is."

"Where?"

"The Vickers Place?"

"You and who?"

"Yes, it is loud, I can hear it. Are you OK? Coppers around? Security?"

"It will take me 25 minutes at least. Wait there. If it is busy, I am not stopping. You are on your own if there's anyone else around."

"Yes, wait there."

"Look for a black car."

"Yes, it will be my car. They will not pull me over if it is all clean, eh?"

"A white gate? Yes, I will pick you up close to that if it is clear."

"I am on way now. Keep your eyes open and do not panic!"

"Hey Snoop, here boy, be back in a while, sorry boy. We will take a walk later."

Jack placed his dinner plate on the floor. It distracted Snoop, who could handle a nice spicy meal. He gathered his helmet and gear and left the house. The last fingers of sunlight were scraping across the rooftops as Jack started his motorcycle and headed out of his driveway. After an uneventful journey through the village and deserted streets, Jack arrived at his lock up. A small garage with a steel roll-up door. Jack dismounted from his motorcycle with the engine running. He unlocked the garage door, secured by a combination lock. He entered the code with care: one, one, zero, seven. Jack looked around and ensured that no-one else was around to observe before pushing the door upwards to open it to its full extent.

Inside the lockup sat Jack's car, a polished 1990 black BMW 325i, caught and illuminated by a single ray of the setting sun. Jack got into the car and grabbed a set of keys from under the passenger seat. He punched them into the ignition and turned. The car started and with a deep growl; the engine purred. Jack drove the car out of the lockup and exchanged positions with the motorcycle. The closed roller door secured with the combination lock. He checked that all the lights on his car were working and then drove off.

The red glow from the instrument panel highlighted the interior of the car and Jack's face. The sun had now disappeared below the horizon. It was dark apart from the light spilling from windows of the homes that lined the deserted street.

"Everyone is watching the game, enjoying a bit of quiet." Said Jack, he mumbled and reached towards the radio and tuned it to the live football commentary.

"A big night and a big game to see who gets to the final in five days. It is make or break time out there it is like a pressure cooker without a lid. Both teams are out on the pitch and acknowledge the support of the crowd of the parts of the crowd that support them." The commentator announced.

Jack drove towards his destination and into the darkness.

20
DRIVER

D arkness is a realm that to some invites fear, to others it joins them as their friend and ally, covering with its heavy blanket all activities that need to remain hidden. It was dark. The roadway was clear, the sparkle of a new frost was forming on the surface of the black asphalt, catching stray particles of light, holding them for a moment and dispersing them like glitter. The distant grumble of a fast car alerted the wildlife to take cover in the adjacent ditches and hedgerows.

Twin tungsten headlights cut through the night, illuminating, and distorting the branches and foliage of intersecting trees as the light brushed its way through them. Forming, for a moment, elongated twisted shadows into a transient woven tunnel. Focused on the road ahead, Jack drove on. There were three miles to go. He felt the road beneath the car as he pushed its limits through bends to assess the amount of grip available between the tires, its surface of the asphalt. In case he needed to drive hard, harder than he was. Tires chirped as for a moment they lost traction, Jack smiled.

His route, planned in his mind as he first left his lock-up, took him past the Poachers, a local pub. Jack knew the pub would show the game and noted as he passed that inside a good-sized crowd had gathered. It reminded him that maybe he should have met Neil rather than expecting to have a quiet evening.

No time to dwell, Jack refocused on what lay in front of him. The country lane unwound its curves like an untamed serpent. He liked this part, driving; he felt the grip of the tires slip as the car twitched again. Reducing his speed, he lowered the side window. In the distance he heard the undulating, high-pitched, bone jarring sound of an alarm. He was close.

Its own monument, the Vickers warehouse, was a solitary, enormous steel paneled building within its own grounds. The windowless walls gave the structure a ghostly presence, with no sign of life from its interior. Its monolithic rectangular outline drew a clear frame against the darkness beyond.

The owners of the business secured the building and its grounds with strong gates, high chain-link fences, barbed wire, floodlights, and an outdated alarm system. For good measure, a security firm patrolled the premises at random, they, or the police, now alerted by the alarm system could be only minutes away. The prize stored inside expected to be electronic goods imported from Asia and new to the English market. A petty thief's dream, goods easily stored and disposed.

The building was a magnet for local thieves. If they were fortunate, they would get away with what they came for. The robbers would off-load their goods to black-market vendors who would trade the stolen products with their preferred retail partners. Pubs and bars were their venues for the 'exclusive' deals that they offered. The most recent example was a load of brand-new video machines. They stole them at the end of November, just in time for the holiday season. The in-demand machines earned those who got hold of them a tidy sum, as they sold like hot cakes at half the retail price. Many grateful local children became acquaintances of a mustached small Italian plumber and his platforms that Christmas.

As Jack approached his target, the intense illumination of his headlights reflected off a pair of tall white industrial gates on his right. The gates were closed; a heavy chain and padlock joined them at the center, still locked them together. Jack knew he was at the pickup point outside the Vickers warehouse. He slowed the car but did not stop, but continued at a walking pace for a distance enough to place him away from the gate. He stopped dead, dimmed the headlights, and checked the horizon in front and through the rearview mirror. It was dark in both directions, he could see no other lights, no one else was on the roads. He relaxed, there was no sign or sound of any activity other than the blaring of the alarm.

He got out of the car to get a better view and walked a few paces in front and then behind. The alarm from the warehouse continued to warble and scream. It was loud, it must have been at least 85 decibels, the point at which sound does some damage, it was no surprise that Jack's ears hurt. He returned to the car and got back in and raised the side window to dull the sound. He took time to turn the vehicle around to face the way he arrived. Moving at a slow speed he returned to the gates before coming to a halt beside them.

No sooner had he stopped the car when two figures emerged from the hedgerow in front and to the left of the vehicle. The figures, both men, were each carrying a large box. Jack knew them, it was Crumb and Spud, two local rogues, both well known to the law as they had involved themselves in crime since their early teens. Spud was a tall, dark, well-built guy in his early twenties, the strong silent type. He had grown up quick, faster than his emotions; he had to, the eldest of four children, Spud's father was an alcoholic and did nothing to support his mother, him, or his siblings. Spud resorted to petty crime to help his family. Now he was in the big time, robbing the Vickers warehouse. Crumb was smaller, having many traits that were the opposite of Spud. He was blond, gaunt, and skinny. He was a follower and had attached himself to Spud since they were at school together, when they had bothered to attend, that is. Crumb liked to talk, he could talk himself out, or into any situation he needed to.

Spud was the first to the car. Jack reached under the dashboard and popped the trunk. Spud loaded his box, followed by Crumb who did the same. They both got into the car in a hurry, Spud in the rear and Crumb in the front passenger seat.

"Jack! Freaking go, go the alarm, the alarm, you must be able to hear that for a good distance. Get us out of here, fast." Said Crumb with urgency.

"Calm down. We are the only car on the road, I am going to drive steady, no panic. That way we will not stand out to anybody and I will not end up in a ditch. The roads are a nightmare, super slippery. I will drop you at the Poachers, going the long way out, back the way I came. It is not the shortest or quickest route because that is exactly where they will not care to stake out, they always look the other end of this lane first." Said Jack as he flicked the headlights back on to illuminate the roadway and pressed the accelerator.

"Hey, that is why you are the man." Crumb said now in a calmer voice.

Jack wanted to figure out what had happened and what the situation was and why were they stranded there, in the middle of nowhere with no transport.

"How were you going to get away? Where is your ride, anyway?" Jack asked Crumb.

"He got spooked when Spud set off the alarm." Crumb said as he looked over his shoulder. There was a moment of silence as Spud considered his response and if he was going to make one. The ongoing radio commentary filled the silence with a shout.

"What a pass. That ball had more flavor than a festive edible fruit platter on a silver plate."

"So, he was just going to leave you there?" Said Jack. He raised his eyebrows as he spoke.

"Yes, no balls. That idiot is in for a spanking when we catch up with him. He was off like the clappers as soon as the alarm went. Wait until Spud gets a hold of him! He will mangle him up for sure."

After a while Spud figured out what to say and raised his hand before speaking as though he was in class waiting for recognition.

"Idiot I am. I cut the wrong wire. But we got the goods, didn't we? Jack the man is here, and we are away. Jobs a good un. What is the score then?"

He added the question to divert attention from the mistake, then using his raised hand to point at the radio before pulling at his ear.

"Nil, nil." Said Jack.

"Not missed much then." Spud added.

"I wanted to watch this game, not be your driver for the evening. The radio is not the freaking same as watching it with a cold beer. I was having a nice quiet night with a beer before you pair called." Said Jack. He raised his voice to answer.

"Hey, calm down, man. You are the man, you know, you are the man." Crumb tried to steady the conversation and take the heat out of the moment.

"Tell you, I am color blind, I can't tell red from green." Spud interjected, he stared at the red glow of the instrument panel and pulled at his ear.

"You cannot tell red from freaking green! And there you are, cutting wires! Unbelievable!" Jack laughed.

"That alarm made me crap myself. It is super loud. You know that noise has made me deaf in this ear. It is ringing like crazy." Spud said, sounding concerned and pulling his ear harder than before. The car sped onwards through the dark and still deserted country lane.

"Just hope it was worth it. What did you nick in there, anything worth your risk?" asked Jack.

"A nice bunch of fireworks." Spud responded, boasting.

"Freaking fireworks!" Jack said, his foot hit the brake pedal, and the car slowed for a moment, jerking everybody forward in their seats. The radio commentary cut in again.

"It looked for sure that shot was heading in, but the keeper got his toes to it like an octopus on a hot plate."

"Yeah, two dozen, top grade Chinese bangers they are, they will be worth taking down the pub after all this has blown over, you will see. Fifty notes each, easy." Crumb said with biased over optimistic confidence.

"Who is going to buy fireworks from you pair? You will be lucky to make a ton for the lot at the most!" Jack said, shaking his head.

"You will see. These are professional grade top quality massive, light up the sky for miles they will a perfect display for all the family to enjoy. I bet the Queen uses this stuff." Said Crumb as his hands gestured upwards and outwards to describe an expanding explosion as he speaks.

"The freaking Queen!" Jack said as he pulled the car into the well-lit Poacher pub car park. He stopped, added, "Look, get in the Poachers, it is full to the brim, mingle, watch the game and try not to stand out."

"Hope they have got a slot machine in there." Spud smiled as he spoke.

The radio commentary got loud and interesting.

"He's through the defense, they are on their backs! This is interesting, interesting, very interesting, goaaaaal! What a goal! He was in the right place at the right time, but he might have been elsewhere in a different game at a different venue, serendipity!"

The crowd in the Poachers pub cheered, their silhouettes forming distorted arrangements of arms and legs in the widows. The sound spilled outside as a police car headed towards the warehouse with its blue lights creating a strobe effect.

"Very well done, man." Crumb patted Jack as he spoke.

"Yeah, they are only 45 minutes late. Leave your junk in the car, I will take it. You collect it when things have got quieter." Jack responded. His eyes followed the police car in his rearview mirror as the strobe of its blue light dissipated into the darkness.

"Hey, it is not junk, make sure you secure it when you store it. We will take care of you when we pick them up." Said Spud.

"Yes, thanks Jack, we will be around to collect them, I hope they have a slot machine in there." Said Spud, almost cutting off the end of his sentence as he slammed the car door as he got out of the car.

"Leave it for a couple of days, OK. I cannot lose my job over something as stupid as this." Said Jack. Now buzz off.

"Freaking fireworks!" Said Jack as he instructed Crumb. Jack watched on as the pair wandered across the asphalt parking area and entered the pub. He pulled the car towards the blanket of darkness, and drove towards home.

21
STUDY

Most of the buildings in the City center enjoyed some architectural character or classic design element, either historic or modern. However, the austere biscuit façade of the building in front of Jack breathed 1960 eastern European block. A gray building that cast a gray shadow, even in the brightest of light. Jack was in Sheffield, England, it was September 1992, and the beginning of the new university year. Constructed during an era of urban rehabilitation, the six-story building appeared after the second world war. The site had been made available after heavy bombing had destroyed over three thousand buildings in the city. It was a raid of December 1940 that caused the heaviest damage and a single, misguided bomb had removed the previous structure from the site. The intended target, the adjacent Ponds Forge steel plant, remained undamaged.

Concrete was the material of the moment and of choice, molded in box forms, replacement buildings thrown together as fast as possible. The construction used prefabricated reinforced concrete panels welded together with town planning ideologies. All proven a monumental failure for the community in the years to come. The resultant design had little regard to anything other than providing habitable space. The harsh exterior of the structure had not weathered well. After over fifty years, the exposed concrete surface had become pitted and worn, eroded by the elements, invaded with a living carpet of moss, and blackened by soot. The building, like an aged face, showed its wrinkles, but they were not laugh lines. Jack removed a letter from his coat pocket and checked out the street number of the location to which it directed him. It matched the address on the front of the building; the town planning university at 6A Pond Street.

"Not quite what I had imagined." Said Jack, sighing as he recalled his daydream and observed groups of unenthusiastic students swallowed whole by main entrance to the building.

Slumped cross-legged, his back against the doorway, sat a bedraggled bearded man, homeless. The man held a cloth cap in his right hand. The cap was there to receive any contribution passed, although with other distractions in mind most students ignored his position. Around his neck and attached to a length of string, knotted at both ends, hung a cardboard handwritten board that read 'FALKLANDS VETERAN'. It was a plea to provide and to recognize service. Jack dug into his pocket and grabbed a handful of coins. He dropped them into the veteran's almost empty cap and nodded. The man smiled in appreciation. Jack thought, not the most valuable location to do such business. Even with the high footfall, he knew students had little in the way of surplus funds at their disposal. He hoped his contribution would go towards something positive and not end in the hand of a street drug dealer.

Jack entered the interior of the building and gazed around. In a strange way, it was not a disappointment. The walls of the entrance hall matched the dull garb of the exterior, dull, and gray. The walls encased a crowd of students waiting to make their way to class, huddled towards a small elevator door. Jack looked at the display on his wristwatch, 08:55. The letter unfolded again to confirm the class location and start time:

9AM — AN INTRODUCTION TO TOWN PLANNING. LECTURE ROOM 7F (7th Floor).

Jack moved into the student group. The elevator door slid open and through no choice of his own found himself pushed to the rear wall of the elevator. He could not see the operating panel, let alone access the push button.

"Seven please" Said Jack, hoping one of the other students would press the button to start the launch sequence to the top floor.

The doors closed. Jack recalled the elevator disaster at his office and shuddered. He avoided all eye contact and hoped that none of the others in the confined space were claustrophobic and that the elevator would not get stuck. After a brief wait, the elevator creaked and groaned as it started its journey upwards, pausing at each floor to disgorge a portion of its cargo. By the time the elevator had reached the seventh floor, Jack was the only one left. It was 09:00; he was late; he was never late; Jack hurried on.

Inside the lecture theater, the student class was ready, waiting and already hushed. Jack hunkered down and sought the first vacant chair he could find. Amongst the sea of faces, found an opening in the second row from the front. He sat and regained his breath. Professor Tresswell entered the room a moment behind him. The professor was a lanky, bearded man in his late 50s. Dressed in a tweed jacket complete with sewn leather elbow pads, he wore the uniform of a man who had studied geography his entire life. Jack looked down at the professor's footwear. He half expected to see a pair of white socks encased in brown sandals. It disappointed him to see a traditional pair of tattered brown brogues.

"Good morning all." Said Professor Tresswell, announcing in a loud voice as he faced the class, his hands gripping the lectern at both sides as he rocked it back and forth.

The students answered as a disorganized melancholy group, "Morning".

The professor continued. He took time to scan around the room as he spoke.

"It's good to see you all here this morning. For those who do not know me, I am Professor Tresswell, and I am your course leader. I have been with the university for over twenty years now. This course, as you all should have comprehended, will take two years to complete and at the end you will have an accredited qualification. A qualification that you can use to get membership of the Royal Town Planning Institute. Very prestigious, from there you will find your career will take off and you will look back on this as the turning point."

"I see that some of you are 'mature' students and will bring a lot of experience in class. I want you to set that aside and start from a position of learning about the foundation of town planning. That will be important." Said Tresswell.

The professor turned to the whiteboard behind him and in front of the class. He wiped off what remained of the notes from a previous lecture and wrote as he spoke.

"So, this first semester we will deal with several foundational subjects, each will be as essential and assessed as part of your final grade." Said the professor.

On the board he wrote:

URBAN SPACE MAKING

RURAL ECONOMY (BLOCK)

PLANNING LAW

SOCIOLOGY

"As the course is two-year part-time, we will schedule full-time 'block-weeks' for certain subjects. It is important that you attend these, as each will focus on a specialized subject or theory. We note the block weeks on your timetables, but we will have exact dates later in the semester as we confirm locations. At least one of the block weeks in the 'Rural Economy' section, held in a location that lends itself to the area of study. Well, those are the basics. Having got through that, I would suggest that for now meet your classmates. Do you have questions?"

Students posed several questions about the timing, content, best textbooks, and other non-remarkable facts that need not be recalled. The only question that struck Jack, and perhaps the rest of the class, asked by Aze. Aze was one of the mature students, like the others he worked full time and could attend the class for one day a week. The block weeks would require attendance for an entire week, sometimes off campus. Well dressed and well fed, Aze was of Pakistani decent and spoke with a broad Yorkshire accent.

"Er, do we have to attend all the block weeks?"

"Yes, they will count for fifty percent of your final grade. They are very important; you will not get a pass from this course of study unless you attend all block weeks." Answered the Tresswell.

"That is heavy, I have responsibilities you know!"

"What sort of responsibilities?" Asked Tresswell.

"Well, I play a lot of cricket, organize most of the club events and do the sandwiches, various fillings you understand, we have vegans, vegies and various sexual denominations. I take care of all of it," Said Aze.

"If you want to get qualified from this course, you will need to put the effort in and find a balance. Maybe get someone else to make the sandwiches." Said the Professor.

"It will affect my bowling, all that note taking and writing."

"Anything else?" Professor Tresswell asked and waited for a response. Not getting any, he said.

"Well, if that is all you have, I suggest you spend the rest of today getting to meet your classmates and the various resources available on campus. I will see you all next week."

Professor Tresswell left the room. Most students, except Jack and those seated around him, packed up their belongings to head out to the university library. The others were Bob, Chris, Aze, Russ, Sandra, Jane, Tony, and Simon. Jack knew that there was no such thing as coincidence and that they had assembled together for a reason. He did not know what the connection was now, but he was sure they would discover it later. Jack offered his introduction.

"Hiya, I am Jack. Hey, let us all go for an early lunch we can get to get to speak to each other better."

"Sounds good. An early lunch, just after 10 in the morning, The Kings Head pub is opposite, perfect." Said Bob.

"The best resource on the campus." Offered Chris.

"That is an old man's pub!" Said Aze.

"You will be fine then." Responded Jack.

The group exited the lecture room and headed for the Kings Head.

22
KINGS

Just thirty-nine steps away from the university building sat the comfortable refuge, 'The Kings Head'. A traditional English pub, ideal in that it met folk law. Thirty-nine steps were the perfect stumbling distance back to the building should an unexpected drinking session ensue.

Unlike its neighbors, this medieval building had survived the destruction of the second world war that cleared all other structures in its vicinity. It stood now, proud and as an outstanding example of real architecture amongst the taller anemic concrete structures that towered beside it, and the modern bus transit station beyond. The converted pub had become a place workers, students, and travelers alike used as a rest stop to talk and pass the time.

The student group had left the university building in a hurry and headed towards the pub. Almost stepping over each another, they entered the pub one by one. Besides Jack, the group comprised nine others; Bob, he was twenty-three and had dark hair and features enhanced by a good example of a five o'clock shadow even though it was mid-morning. Chris was twenty-one and had a full head of blond hair and complementary ruddy complexion, he walked with purpose, it was obvious he did not take any nonsense. Aze was twenty-five and was deep in thought, worried that this course would mean that he may need to put more effort in than he envisioned. Tony was twenty-one, he was taller than the others, and his face supported a pronounced Roman nose. His very introverted manner meant he kept himself to himself. Sandra was twenty-one, a redhead with shoulder length hair, slightly curly hair, which complemented her personality. She could get on with anyone, even if they did not want to get on with her. Robin was twenty-four, and he was off the spectrum, a nerd's nerd. He was always quoting facts and figures with little reason and always carried at least one notebook with him. Simon was twenty-two and was the only southerner of the group and therefore subject to north versus south humor. That did not cause him concern because he had a quick mind and could always offer a scathing comment in response when appropriate, or even when not.

Russ was the oldest of the group at thirty-one and resembled a miniature Tom Jones. His recent marriage was his focus. Russ had a very nervous disposition and would be the last to join in any adventure, if at all. There was Jane who dressed in a new age flowing style tie-dye clothing that matched her sometimes flaky personality, she was the only one of the ten who smoked, she was twenty and had her own opinion about almost anything and was not afraid to share it.

The landlords had decorated the interior of the Kings Head to resemble an Elizabethan Manor, matching the period of the building itself. Jack studied the replica paintings by famous old masters filled the walls. Robin pointed out that the portraits included William Dobson's portrait of King Charles 1, who lost his head in 1649, and therefore more than likely the subject of the name of the pub.

The comforting warm glow of multiple decorative wall lamps illuminated the paintings. Several tables filled the space of the main lounge. An open, blazing fire warmed the space. It was still early in the day, so only a few locals and other students were present, and they sat between various tables and the bar. Jack glanced around the lounge, he noticed that the veteran he passed earlier was now sitting by the open fire, he had gathered enough funds to purchase a pint of beer and a plate of food and was enjoying both, Jack and the veteran exchanged a glance and a nod of recognition straight out of a Victorian novel.

After finding a table large enough to seat them all and ordering various beverages and food at the bar, the students returned to the table to get to know each other.

"It is too quiet in here." Said Aze. Whispering at an appropriately loud volume.

"Yes, we need to stir things up a bit. You may be right being an old man's pub." Said Jack.

"Tell you what, I will put some music on." Chris said as he left his chair.

"Yeah, good idea, I will come with you." Bob said as he too jumped to follow Chris. They headed over to the jukebox.

"Let us pick some stuff that is rare, I'm Bob."

"Yeah, I'm Chris, Nottingham,"

"Chris Nottingham?"

"No, Chris from Nottingham, that is where I work, just over four years now,"

"Oh, got it, nice one. Dinosaur Jr, that will wake them up, I am working in Hull, same as Tony, we share a ride, takes about an hour."

"That is going to be the longest hour of your life!" Said Chris, noting the fact that Tony was not the greatest of conversationalists.

"You will see," said Bob, continuing with raised eyebrows, "just wait until he has had a few beers. You had better watch out,"

The music selection selected, Bob and Chris returned to the table.

"So, where are you lot from? I am from here, Sheffield," Said Aze. He liked to know as much as he could about others' business.

"Well, I'm Sandra and I'm from Leeds, working at Leeds City in their development control section."

"I work in DC too!" Replied Aze, using the professional slang abbreviation.

"Me, too, that is in DC, not Leeds." Said Jack.

"Anyone else in DC?" Aze enjoyed generating his own sub-groups, and he saw an opportunity.

Jane was the only one to raise her hand. "I am in DC, I am Jane, I work here in Sheffield, with Aze."

Aze did not want Jane to be in his special sub-group, she knew too much about him, so he dispensed with that idea.

The group discovers Russ is from Grimsby, Robin is from Derby, and Tony is from Hull and Sandra is from North Yorkshire.

"Simon, is it?" Aze asked.

"Yes, that is me."

"Oh yes, here he is, a soft southern lad!" Said Aze on hearing Simon's accent.

"Yes, not as soft as your head!" Responded Simon.

"This is going to be fun." Added Aze, as he rubbed his hands together.

"So, where in North Yorkshire?" Jack asked Sandra.

"Scarborough, it's a tourist town silent out of season. What about you?

"Yeah, Mansfield, a mining community. My first proper job. I was doing some stuff for myself, messing about with motorbikes and cars. It earned me a bit of cash. I did not want to end up down the pit, that is where all my family and friends ended up. I had a choice, we all do, and so did they."

23
DROP

The mid-day air required a jacket, but the temperature was moderate for the time of year. The sky was a brilliant blue, clear of cloud. Pippi was on her way to visit the nearby graveyard, she pushed the stroller ahead of her and had no inkling that over 600 miles away, in a Sheffield pub, and at this very moment, a random conversation of a group of strangers would set the destiny of her sleeping three-year-old child.

Pippi was thirty-four, blond hair and medium height. She was born and raised in Lysekil, a small coastal town on the west coast of Sweden and close to Gothenburg, where she lived alone with her daughter Freda. Every Friday, just after lunch, they set out on the journey from her small apartment to the graveyard on the edge of town. Freda would sleep, the motion of the stroller acting as a soothing blanket and a full belly adding to her comfort. On the way Pippi would stop at the florists in the square to buy flowers, two bunches of whatever was in season. Today she only purchased one. Required so she could tend to a specific grave and headstone. In the grounds, there were two graves she could visit, today she would only visit one.

Her brisk walk brought her beside the Lysekil caviar packing factory, a two-story brick warehouse building. The caviar export business was an activity that had gone on there for over one-hundred years, Pippi continued past the docks next to the factory, she would always note the boats that moored there. Today a large freighter, the 'Gyllene Agget' was busy loading its cargo. She remembered the name. The same freighter was there at most of the times she passed, loading up crates and barrels. She watched as workers scurried around the dock as the crane operators grabbed multiple pallets from the factory wharf and lifted them, swinging onto the deck of the boat. Pippi glanced up at the ship. She noticed a single figure leaning on the guard rail of the upper deck of the boat closest to her direction. A tall man in a long overcoat, she thought for a moment that he would wave, but he did not, he seemed to shrug and shuffle his feet. Pippi walked on.

It was still some distance to her destination. The well-worn path caused the stroller to shake as it rolled, Freda was undisturbed and continued to sleep. The path led past a low stone boundary wall, stained brown over time by exposure to the salt water and sea air. A sign attached to the wall announced the graveyard entrance was ahead. Meeting that point, she knew she was fifty yards away from her destination. A stone arch marked the entrance to the graveyard, outlining the shape of a pair of open wrought-iron gates.

Pippi made her way through the archway and turned towards a headstone that was located away in a distant corner of the yard. Freda was still sleeping, and Pippi hoped she would stay so while she tended to her business.

The stone tended well, clean, and identified with an inscription, 'ERIK HOLM 1944-1965, BELOVED SON AND BROTHER'. At the base of the stone, a small dark porcelain vase held a fresh arrangement of flowers. Pippi murmured but remained asleep, Pippi parked the stroller beside the grave. She looked at the inscription on the stone and lingered on it. She felt no sadness until she glanced over at a unique stone on the other side of the graveyard.

As she moved toward the stone in front of her to kneel, she stumbled, and with an instinct pushed out a hand to save her fall. She disturbed the vase which tipped, spilling the fresh-cut flowers it contained onto the ground beside the gravestone. She looked down; the vase acted as a lid to a hole which revealed its opening. She knew what it concealed, so unsurprised, Pippi checked no one had seen, there was no other in the graveyard, so she continued. Pippi sat upright, brushed off her gloved palm and with straightened fingers plunged it into the hole and probed for what it contained.

She felt the package was there, as she expected. It was a perfect fit for the cavity it occupied. With some difficulty and having removed one glove, Pippi maneuvered her fingers in the space to grasp the compact, wrapped bundle. She glanced around again in all directions. No one else was there. With some effort, she squashed and squeezed the package to daylight and freedom.

Pippi sat back on her haunches and held up the packet to inspect it. It was the same size as a regular envelope, but of a thickness of a house brick and sealed with strong tape. After setting the package to one side, she replaced the vase and set inside the new flower arrangement that she had bought with her.

She picked up the packet. she took out her pocketknife to cut through the tape. It opened; Pippi flicked her finger across the edge of a wad of banknotes. The contents were consistent to what they had always been when she had collected the drop on earlier occasions. She passed the Gyllene Agget, her eyes directed towards the top deck. The man was no longer there. Pippi continued past the docks, the freighter, and the factory towards the town. Freda murmured and became restless. Time to get home.

Pippi felt the weight of the package in her pocket and knew that she would return to the graveyard in a week to collect the same.

24
CAVIAR

A bustling activity described the loading deck of the Gyllene Agget. Dockworkers and deckhands scurrying back and forth like worker bees feeding their queen, each knowing their place within the melee. Wooden shipping crates stacked in leaning towers sat on the dockside, each crate branded on its side with the words 'LYSEKIL SPECIALITY CAVIAR' and a reference number. Customs clearance paperwork stapled on their sides fluttered in the gusts rolling off the water. Amongst the crate's large barrels of fish oil, an export to destinations throughout Europe. Both the caviar and fish oil were products that the area had produced for hundreds of years. The caviar had a unique recipe of cod roe, canola oil, sugar, onion, tomato sauce, salt, and a hint of dill. It was still one of the most popular sandwich spreads in the country and was enjoying increased demand from overseas.

Built in 1983, the Gyllene Agget was a ship of a type known as a reefer. It was so designed to carry goods and freight such as foodstuffs, which required a temperature-controlled environment. The cargo today, a similar quantity of crates and barrels as seen at this location on certain days of the week. The crates were being loaded in a hurry by the pivoting on-board derreck lifting gear as they hurried to meet the programmed departure time, just before dusk.

Set to sail in a few hours, the passage from Lysekil to Hull in England, would take the vessel just over two days. If the weather permitted, as it should if the outlook held as the forecast broadcast earlier suggested. Dogger, Fisher, German Bight, southeast veering southwest 2 or 3, occasionally 4 later. Showers. Moderate or good. A radio weather forecast, in a format which noted the sea areas, described the wind direction and speed, the conditions and visibility of the route. It measured the force of the wind on a scale of 0 up to 14, so 2 to 3 meant that the outlook was not too bad.

The uppermost deck of the boat was empty apart from a non-crew member, a passenger. A fine suit and a long trench coat defined the tall man. His appearance and the texture of his skin bore no wear common to the seafaring type. This was true, he was not looking forward to the passage over the hostile North Sea at all, his violent sea sickness would confirm that at the first opportunity. He preferred road or rail transport for long journeys, but that was not an option in his present circumstance. The passenger was familiar with the boat as he had sailed with the vessel and its cargo from its previous destination. A very unenjoyable three-day voyage from Hamburg, Germany. He had arrived in Lysekil with the ship on Wednesday, disembarked for business and had reappeared not long afterwards to rejoin the vessel. The passenger kept himself to himself, his business was his business, he dealt in a known trade, a trade not discussed in casual conversation.

The desk at the highest point of the boat afforded him a complete panoramic view of the town. Seagulls circled the town square area, and he could hear their squawking echoes as they squabbled over a scrap of food they had found, like a punctured bagpipe. Small homes raised up their red roofs on the hillside that lay beyond. He looked out with a recognition and nostalgia, every now and again concentrating on a particular building or landmark. A movement directed his focus towards the town's graveyard, and toward a single figure, pushing a stroller at pace. He watched in silence. There was a moment of guilt, but he would offer no sympathy and it was not his want to display nor ask for any. His hand searched his jacket pocket and grasped a small, cold metal object. It was a wedding ring, too small to fit on any of his fingers. He played with it for a while.

"Mr. you are ready?" A deckhand interrupted the moment.

"Oh Yes, let's go, do you have my luggage?"

"Yes, the cases are in your cabin as you asked." Said the deckhand.

"Ok, thank you. I will follow you."

As the last crate of caviar loaded into the hold of the freighter, the cranes returned to their stations, and the two stepped below.

25
HELIUM

Some weeks had passed, the days had become shorter in light, the town planning course had ground on, and the student group had got to know each other much better. After the term break, the second semester of the course was about to start. The students had reconvened and today, Friday afternoon, was the first lecture in the rural economy module, the module that would irrevocably connect some students to others far away. The group waited for the lecture to start, sharing life event updates as they waited.

Gradually the catchup chatter dissipated, and all eyes settled to focus on the diminutive figure who had arrived in a whisper at the front of the class. Well, maybe only on the upright hair on the head of that figure. Cherie Rosebud was only inches taller than the podium from which she stood behind. They well knew Cherie in her profession and had been lecturing on this subject for twenty years. Her voluminous bohemian dress reflected her personality, high energy, nervous, fidgety, and full of air.

"Hello everybody I am Cherie Rosebud and for those that do not know me I'm your lecturer for the rural economy module today we will discuss the process by which all or even more of that most places by that I mean communities attempt to control and or design the change and the development in their environments is all urban planning." Cherie started the lecture. With no pause for breath until the moment she had exhaled the entire volume of her lungs, she quickly followed that with a loud intake of air as though she had been underwater for two minutes.

"Now, I am going to be right in thinking that this is going to be a cracker." Said Bob, in the gap between Cherie's breaths, and before she continued.

"Town planning is the art of shaping and guiding the physical yes physical growth of the town creating buildings and environment to meet the various needs of the society such as social cultural economic recreational business and vocational and to build a community."

As Cherie delivered the sentence, again as one whole, the tone of her voice transitioned through at least three octaves of increasing pitch, before she again grasped for air with a high whistling breath, Jack was sure that dogs for all around would be disturbed by the screeching sound.

The lecture continued without pause.

"To provide a healthy yes healthy conditions for all and for children to live and work and relax and Town Planning is aimed at us all to bring social and economic well-being of different places different spaces spaces as places and places as spaces let's take a brief look at what we will call policies for place and space or space and place."

At this point Cherie was hyperventilating, and she took an additional sharp intake of breath.

"It is swings and roundabouts as to which is the best, place or space." Remarked Chris. A distracted Jack thought for a moment and then interjected, "Hey, just remembered, my cousin 'Udde' will visit me next week. I'll ask him to stop by, it's a block week."

Cherie, her face now a shade of bright pink, had replenished her tank and continued with the lecture.

"Beauty yes beauty to allow us to preserve and experience the remarkable individuality of the town by developing it in the most natural conditions through flexible sustainable elements of design yes design to control all pieces of the town and country all the principles."

Udder? Really? Udder? Questioned Chris, in the now regular interval where Cherie would fill her lungs to reach maximum capacity.

"It's spelt U. D. D. E. and pronounced hue — der. And Er, oh, he is from Sweden, yes Sweden."

"So towns and cities are where people live yes live and work or work and live and the people living in them and places and spaces are the places and spaces that people are most of the time if not all the time working or living. But what about the rural locations is that work and no play or play and no work."

"Told you. A cracker." Confirmed Bob.

"Sweden?" Asked Chris.

"Yes, Sweden, er, near Gothenburg, yes a town near Gothenburg, I recall." Replied Jack as they all became more preoccupied with the content of the ongoing conversation than the lecture.

"Sweden? So, you have Swedish relatives?" Chris continued with his line of questioning before Cherie started again.

"More than that oh much more than buildings I'm speaking about the spaces that fill the places the streets the roads the people don't forget the people the children yes the children playing in the streets where do they play in the villages the fields and the farms where do they get their clothes."

Cherie reached the highest note yet and needed a very sharp intake of breath.

"I think she's on helium, must be helium." Said Bob.

Jack continued with the previous conversation.

"Yes, I did some research, and I came back with some Swedish links from my mom's side and found some contacts over there. Pure luck. I had no inkling that I even had any more cousins, well when I say cousin, I think he is a second cousin."

"The children on the porches playing in the streets the parks their smiling faces their future is the places that we will build not with bricks but with empty spaces filled with children and people sitting on the porches many porches with steps to open doors at the top families and activity and joy in the streets."

"So, I contacted Udde by email a while ago, and just by chance he is visiting the UK next week. He has agreed to come up here as he will be close-by. It is a block week so I can meet him. Probably in the Kings Head at lunch."

"How long is he here?" Sandra had overheard the discussion and had decided that it was impossible to keep up with what Cherie was speaking about.

Jack looked around the class, taking time to think before he said.

"Oh, Um, next week, I think. He works in telecoms and has meetings in the City to do with his job, anyway."

"So, next week? what day?" Sandra enquired.

"Er, yeah, Wednesday, I think. I need to confirm with him." Said Jack.

"We all get to meet him?"

"Oh, sure, I think he should be OK with him. He knows all about you guys." Said Jack, just before Cherie's last words of the day.

"With the landscape rolling into the sea." Cherie closed her lecture with a sharp intake of breath. The students sat in silence for a moment before reacting.

"I do not know about you guys, but I need a drink after this crap." Sandra said with a shrug.

Jack turned to Bob and shook his head. "Bob, this is just pipe-tastic, my ears are bleeding."

"Helium, no doubt about it!" Said Bob in confirmation.

26
UDDE

Lunchtime on the following Wednesday had arrived without consequence. The group traced the thirty-nine steps as they did on a regular occasion towards the Kings Head, anticipating their meeting with Udde, Jack's cousin. Jack now had to face what he had sown. It was not to be as everyone had expected, and they would soon discover the plot. Jack had everything in place and amazed that no one in the group had questioned the fact that he had been carrying a small package around with him all morning. He was still uncertain how the event would play out.

The group entered the pub; it was lunchtime and busy. They were in luck as the table that they would use on lunchtime visits was available. Bob claimed the table, and the group arranged themselves in their regular positions. Jack placed the bundle under his chair and went to the bar with the others to order lunch, Chris was already there.

"Right, I will have a pint of bitter and a pie, please." Said Chris to the barman.

"I will have the same." Said Jack, chiming in.

The group having ordered their sustenance returned to the table, around it in a clockwise order were Jack, Sandra, Jane, Russ, Tony, Aze, Simon, Bob, and Chris.

"I'm curious." Said Jack, who timed his words to a moment at which the whole of the group would hear.

"About what?" Asked Sandra.

"Well, I know little about you guys, but I think we all have novel ideas about what we would like to be doing. I mean, rather than going through this. Where is it that each of us wants to get to? Or is this your ambition?" Said Jack.

"What do you mean?" Asked Chris.

"You know, in twenty, thirty years, what do you expect to have done, achieved? You must have had something that may differ from town planning?"

"Well, I am going to be running a jazz bar!" Said Jane without hesitation.

"Jazz! There is no point to that racket, I cannot say how you could ever describe that junk as music. I have heard more melody in a food blender full of spoons." Said Chris.

"Better than what you guys put on the jukebox here." Said Jane and continued. "Go on then, what's your ambition, Chris?

"Oh yes, I am going to be living with an Australian soap star or two and thrilled with that I tell you."

"We are trying to be serious here, Chris," Said Sandra.

"I am serious, you will see. Me and Kylie will do just fine. Kylie, and yes, I am talking about the princess of pop."

"Dreamy". Said Jane, scoffing at the thought, and continued.

"Oh well, we would all like to see that. So, Bob, what about you? Any soap stars in your future?"

"Rock-and-roll. In my band. Doing gigs and working on a number one record. Should have done it when I was younger when I had the chance." Said Bob.

"In a band, eh?" Asked Sandra.

"Yeah, well, I used to be in one before this. We ran out of money, and ideas, but, we did not get a break, we were not bad though. Hey, Tony, what is your ambition?

"Er, don't have one." Hesitated Tony.

"What about you, Jack?" Sandra picked up the conversation.

"I think I would like to have written a movie script by then."

"What about?" Enquired Sandra.

"Not sure, about all of this, I think! None-one will believe it though."

"The one thing that will happen is that I'm going to be captain of the local cricket club and the best-off spinner they've ever seen." Interjected Aze.

"And that is the part no-one will believe." Said Jack.

"You need to turn up for that Aze! Anyway, Jack, where is your cousin? Is he coming? Asked Bob.

"I am waiting for him to call. I told him where we would be." Jack said as he glanced at his mobile phone and then looked around the pub. He knew it was time for his plan.

"But he's not messaged or anything. Maybe I will take a quick look outside, to see if I can spot him if he's lost and wandering around out there." Said Jack.

Jack picked up the small bag from under his chair and left the table, passing through the pub and out of sight of the group. He turned into the men's bathroom, which was located close to the rear exit of the pub. Close by, sitting at a table enjoying their lunch were two regular customers, a pair of workers from a nearby warehouse. As Jack entered the bathroom, the door closed behind him and one of the worker's commented to the other.

"He is in a bit of a hurry, must be a bad pint lad."

"Yes, seen that look many a time. Off to trap two, I bet." Added the second.

The bathroom was empty. He knew because he had checked every stall by pushing on each door to open it and had received no surprises in return. Fortune being with him, he stood at the sink and opened the small bag that contained a blond wig. This was the start of his plan.

Plan in this context being an unplanned action or course of events. For whatever reason, he could not determine why, maybe boredom, who knew? He had concocted the scheme with no preconception. A Swedish cousin? Why would he suggest such a thing? His most remote relative was Aunt Glenda, who lived in Northampton, only sixty miles away, and she was of pure English descent.

But there he was, standing in a bathroom staring into a mirror and hoping that no-one would come in. Jack took a deep breath and positioned the wig on his head. It was of a length that was long enough to cover his dark hair, but short enough so it did not quite reach his shoulders. He had obtained the wig from his sister-in-law. She did not ask why, and he had appreciated that. He studied his reflection in the mirror. The wig was too perfect, he realized, so he roughed it up with his fingers before splashing on some water for greater messiness. It worked, he looked like a corn field scarecrow lost in mid-winter. He removed his jacket and turned it inside out so that the dark sheen of its liner replaced the blue checks of its outer.

"Yes, that is perfect,"

Jack became Udde and practiced his very poor Swedish accent.

"Hey der I ham der Udde from Sveeeden."

"How der everboody doin' in todais."

"That works."

Jack exited the bathroom to a comment of "Bloody Hell" from one worker who had seen him enter moments before. "Must have been some heavy stuff!" added the other before he continued his lunch.

'Udde' wandered back into the bar and through it for a while. He arrived at the table where the group was sitting and from where he had departed only minutes before. Jack was sure that the scheme would be up in a matter of seconds. They would recognize him, and it would end as a bit of a laugh, something that would make the day more enjoyable, perhaps.

"Hey, dis is der table vor were Jaq is? You all are da planink peopol?" Jack returned to character and asked the group.

"Yes, he has just gone outside to look for you!" Replied Russ. He was nervous, this was a stranger. He did not feel comfortable with new people.

"You must have passed him outside." Said Aze.

What? They did not recognize him! Jack now saw the opportunity to take this further.

"I comink on der bous, and this has nothing in der power for der foner."

"Oh, so your phone is dead?" Said Russ.

"Ja, ja, ja, the dead door mousey as der phone."

Russ nodded. The unfamiliar situation justified his nervousness.

"So, der, you moost be der larger than big Azey!" Said Udde as he pointed to Aze.

"You, cheeky bastard, what has Jack been saying then?"

"Only gooood, you play bat the ball and eat good of food."

Jack struggled to maintain the character and in time all around the table caught on to the disguise, all except Russ. The conversation continued between the two.

"Ruus, are the wifey good with you in here?"

"Yes, she is…" Said Russ. He hesitated and then rocked backwards on his chair as the realization hit him.

"It is him; it is Jack!" Said Russ. He pushed backwards from the table in horror until the angle of lean broke equilibrium of balance. Russ fell backwards, holding his beer, which spilled into his face. Russ got to his feet and ran out of the King Head; he found the entire experience very unsettling and disappeared until the following week. The group left the pub laughing, having another story that they could recount as part of any nostalgic return to the days they had spent in the Kings Head.

Jack removed the wig and put Udde away for another time, a time of adventure.

27
CHOICE

A function of finance and political ambition defines the running of a municipal government, the two common but uncomfortable bed fellows. The casualties of internal wrangling of resources are staff held accountable for the management and implementation of policies and the projects they produce.

The planning office was quiet, Jeff was at his desk in the corner office, surrounded by his collection of papers, documents and notes. He was busy making phone calls and in and out of meetings with various finance managers, as had occurred most days this week. The others in the department had noticed that Jeff was at his desk more than normal and seemed ill at ease. In the opposite corner, as far away from Jeff as possible, sat Neil. Silenced, both in sound and action by the unannounced hangover he was carrying from the activity of the previous night. Everybody knew, but no-one asked.

Jack was sitting at his desk in concentration. He was working on the most extensive project of the year, the largest land reclamation and recreation scheme that the town would ever see. Last month the department put together a bid for financial aid based on the parameters of the project. The team highlighted the fact that it would reuse a contaminated site and bring the opportunity for the community to enjoy a new sports facility. Last week the agency confirmed the award of a grant to carry out the work. The requirement came with tight deadlines to complete the plans and to start the work on site. Jack was thinking hard, figuring out the minimum dimensions of the required hockey fields and attempting different arrangements to fit them into the allotted space.

Jack sat up at his drawing board and stretched his back straight. At that moment Angie entered the office. It had been some days since he had seen her; she had not been around as much, and he had no reason to visit the reprographics room. It was unusual that she would venture into in the planning office anyhow, or even outside of the reprographics room. She smiled, waved at Jack, and signed.

"I owe you dinner."

"Why?" Said Jack, he was not expecting to see Angie, never mind getting a dinner invitation.

"You will not believe this!" Angie smiled and continued. No-one else in the office could understand sign language. The conversation between Jack and Angie was a silent event between them, nobody in the office had a clue to what they were saying.

"I lost my betting ticket, but found it yesterday, I knew I had won with the first two."

"Seventy-five pounds if I recall, right? But keep that and let me buy you dinner." Signed Jack.

"No, you do not understand. Most of the others won too!" Angie motioned with a flourish of hand gestures.

"You what!" Said Jack, signing and jumping off his chair to stand.

"I won thousands!"

Angie took a step forward and hugged Jack, and he hugged her back. They had connected, now there was something between them, he was sure of that.

"Jack!" Said Jeff. He interrupted them with some urgency.

"I need to speak to you, Jack, if you have ten minutes?" Said Jeff. Speaking without the intensity that often-formed part of his conversations.

"I'm free now. Sure." Said Jack, answering Jeff.

"We will speak later about arranging a dinner."

Jack turned and signed to Angie, who then skipped out of the office, still smiling. She peeked back over her shoulder at Jack and smiled again.

"Right, let us go into the conference room." Said Jeff. He signaled and pointed in the room's direction where only serious things happened, hiring, or firing.

"You doing OK? Please close the door."

"Yes, all OK, what is up?"

"Sit down. I must tell you, not good news. Have you learned the budget is being cut?"

"Yes, well, I have heard rumors, but that they said no job cuts through?" Asked Jack. He needed to find out if it would affect him. He felt in his gut that something was not good.

"Oh, well yes, no job cuts from the total number. They have moved some line items around, that includes the training budget for next year. I could do nothing about that, I'm sorry." Said Jeff, concerned that Jack may find him out.

"You are aware, this my last year on the planning course? If I do not complete the course, then it will leave me with nothing." Jack was getting disturbed. There was something that Jeff knew, but was not telling.

"There is always the possibility to get you funded for the following year. But no promises."

"Yes, no promises! In the meantime, I am just hanging around. No promotion then either, I presume. What is the point?" Said Jack, disappointed. His choices were being formed by others, and he did not like any of them.

"Well, no, sorry. The budget is tight. In fact, your position is being moved. The catch is that you will need to apply for it. The position is in strategic planning though."

Jack's heart sank. Strategic planning was as close to working as an accountant as one could get in planning. Only quantity surveying as a profession could be worse. It was monotonous work, no drawing, no creativity, just numbers and statistics. He visualized their office full of gray suited pretend executives.

"Who will finish the reclamation plans?" Said Jack. Demanding to know what the thoughts for his position were.

"We'll push work out to specialist consultants; the cost is less in the long run. It's a money saving thing." Said Jeff in reply before adding.

"I'll give you a positive reference."

"You're aware how it works here Jeff, if your face does not fit then you are out. It is all politics. They have their pet people in strategy. And I bet the consultant is already in mind. You know there is nothing else going on in this town apart from the coal mine. If you think that will be my only choice, you are wrong. I'll not do that. You will see."

A bitter but determined Jack left the room, He would set his own choice no matter what.

28
FIREWORKS

Certain events are of such prominence that just by their occurrence they will etch a permanent memory into the mind of any witness. They are many and varied. People remember the same day for different reasons. A dog's bite, a missed bus, a good meal, a chance meeting, a touch, a perfume, a song, or any of a multitude of other unremarkable events.

What happened on this night will have burned its mark on any of its observers. They will recall the moment for a long time afterwards with some clarity, for it played into their future.

Jack had returned from work, confused. What a day it had been. With a frown, he contemplated the talk with Jeff. He played through in his mind what had happened. The morning had started well, but by the end it had not been a good day. He needed to put together a plan that was his choice, not the whim of the most boring of creatures, a number crunching municipal accountant. Jack's worst nightmare, to be on a path that had no foundation for his future. He could not let that happen. Certain of that; Jack tried to relax and considered his exchange and hug with Angie and imagined a day that they were together, an adventure perhaps. The frown eased for a moment.

A loud, persistent knocking at the front door broke his thought. Snoop barked. Jack opened the door, not knowing the reason for the visit or who the caller might be. On the doorstep, Spud and Crumb, eyes wide, standing side by side, hear no evil, speak no evil.

"Hey Jack." Said Crumb.

"Hey guys. Come for your fireworks, yeah? Go around the back, I put them all in the shed." Said Jack.

"Are you OK? you don't appear to be yourself." Said Crumb, he expected Jack to berate them both for turning up unannounced. He understood something was bothering Jack from the frown on his forehead.

"Yeah, just a bad day at work."

Crumb nodded; Spud shrugged his shoulders; they had never had jobs, so there was little relevance to them both. The three made their way to the rear of Jack's house.

Typical of all the others that made up the row, the rear yard stretched about forty paces from the back of the house. A well-kept lawn surrounded by a few small shrubs and plants in their dying bloom formed the sizable, but narrow, garden. Closest to the house a patio deep enough to park a motorcycle or lay out to catch the sun on the odd days that it appeared. A knee-high brick wall separated the paved area from the garden. At the far end of the lawn sat a small wooden shed. A solid timber fence, tall enough to require an average person to stand on tip toes to see over, established the full extent of the yard and maintained a barrier to its neighbors.

"They are in the shed, in there." Said Jack as he pointed to his garden shed. Spud was busy smelling the remains of a dead flower he had discovered.

"Leave that alone, Spud." Said Crumb. "It is only a Dandelion; it is a weed!"

"Weed? Can you smoke it then?". He crushed the dead leaves between his fingers and sniffed again. He sneezed.

"Do not be a dozy twonk!" Said Crumb. "Come on, let us get on with it."

Jack got to the shed first. He held the lock on the shed door, and dialed in the combination, concealing the sequence as he did so.

"They better not be soggy. If we can't use them because they've got damp, then they'll be worthless. Nothing is worse than a damp firework." Said Crumb.

"They'll be OK. It is weatherproof and its as dry as your underwear in there and we have had a few warm days." Said Jack.

"Damp underwear, that is much worse. I know that." Said Spud, pulling at the rear of his pants.

"I do not think my pants are weatherproof."

Crumb was becoming frustrated with Spud's random commentary. Jack could not help but smile as he opened the shed door. The frown cast off for a moment. Jack had stacked the two boxes of fireworks under an old blanket at the back of the shed.

"There they are, at the back."

"We should test one." Said Crumb.

"What? Here?" Said Jack concerned, he did not think his backyard would be the proper testing venue place for a stolen product. And anyway, the news reports the previous evening had warned that a batch of stolen industrial strength fireworks were in circulation, and for the public to stay away from them and report any suspicious activity.

"Yeah, no point in trying to sell them on if they are all duds. Go on, get one out then." Said Crumb, gesturing to Spud to enter the shed.

"There are no spiders in there, are they?" Asked Spud?

"Just get one out!"

After the sound of rustling and movement of garden equipment subsided, Spud emerged from the shed. In his hand was a single firework. It was not quite what Jack had expected. A large sphere, a small globe, attached to a tube the size of a milk carton. Connected to its side was a stick, double the length of its body. A small piece of fuse protruded from the underside. Wrapped around the side of the explosive, a logo depicting a bright green fire breathing Chinese dragon.

"That is crazy huge! How are you going to set that off?" Said Jack. He knew that this was not a good idea.

"Let me look at the instructions, No way! Look, they are all in Chinese!" Said Crumb, as he took hold of the firework before handing it back to Spud in disgust.

"Hey, I could hold it like this." Said Spud. He held the firework upright by its stick at arm's length.

"Don't be a dozy twonk, it will blow your hand off. We can use the stick to stand it in a tube or a bottle or something." Said Crumb, recalling the method his parents used to launch rockets when he was a child.

"This must be the fuse." Said Spud, as he pulled at the tiny string affixed to the underside of the firework.

"Jack, do you have a bottle then?" Asked Crumb.

"There should be one in the shed."

"Go on then Spud, fetch one out." Said Smurf with some urgency.

Spud re-entered the garden shed and re-appeared with an empty bottle. Here you go; this will do. It is a good job Jack drinks the fancy stuff, as he read aloud the label on the bottle, "Spirit of Turpentine. Is that French then?"

"Never mind that. Stand it upright in the ground over there." Said Crumb.

Spud planted the bottle into the soft ground and placed the stick of the rocket into its neck. It stood upright, just.

"There you are, steady as a rock. Jack you do the honors mate."

"There's no freaking way that I'm going anywhere near that with a naked flame."

"Well, someone has to! And I will. Who has got a light?" Said Spud.

"Not me." Said Jack.

"I don't." Said Crumb. "We need a freaking spark from somewhere! Jack, get an old newspaper, roll it up and light it on the stove-top in your kitchen. And you better settle your dog away, Jack. There's going to be a rumble."

Jack and Spud entered the kitchen and re-emerged, Spud holding a rolled-up sheet of newspaper, flaming at its tip. Spud marched towards the firework carrying the newspaper with arm outstretched. Jack jumped behind the patio wall and peered over the top. Crumb climbed onto the roof of the garden shed and looked down over the ridgeline. Without hesitation Spud pushed the newspaper and flame under the base of the rocket and the fuse ignited with a splutter.

"Freaking heck." Said Jack.

Spud turned to run towards the patio. He had four yards to make up. Two steps later, the fuse smoked, ignited the propellant, and the rocket launched into the evening sky. The object reached an altitude just higher than the roof of the shed, about fifteen feet, stopped and hung there for what seemed like minutes. Their eyes focused on the same point in the sky. A rocket suspended in time.

"It is a dud." Said Crumb, from his position on top of the shed.

Spud managed another half a step before the rocket exploded. It was still silent. An enormous ball of intense bright light filled the sky. Jack looked at Spud and was sure that he saw him as an x-ray against the brilliant illumination. The silence soon followed by what witnesses have only been able to describe as a sonic boom. Still holding the flaming newspaper, Spud half leapt, and half fell over the patio wall and landed face down on the concrete. The violent sound surprised Crumb, and he fell from the roof of the garden shed onto his back.

"Hiro freaking, shima!" Said Jack, with a gasp.

The blast caused windows to vibrate, car alarms to sound, and dogs to bark. Neighbors left their dinner tables to venture outside to investigate. After a few seconds of silence, Spud got to his feet.

"Blimey, that was bright, was it red or green?" He asked.

"We can't take those down to the pub, they'll blow someone's bloody head off." Said Crumb. Picking himself up from the rear of the shed and brushing away the debris.

"And you say the Queen uses these? You pair better get out of here before someone puts their teeth back in and reports all this." Said Jack.

29
DESTINATION

P rofessor Tresswell stood in front of a hushed lecture hall. The students waited in anticipation. Today, they will find out the destination for the block week. They had been looking forward to this since the start of the course. To some it had come down to two probable locations, one of them being London. No one had put together the fact that the subject of study was entitled 'The Rural Economy' and London was not in fact anywhere close to being rural. Identification of the other possible location was still a mystery, but if London was a favorite to be one, the alternative should be desirable.

"Here we go, we will find out where we are off to this year." Said Bob.

"Somewhere that involves some action, we will need it with Tresswell there." Said Chris.

"I am not too bothered. My work told me last week they will not be funding this course for next year." Said Jack.

"What does that mean? That you are out?" Asked Chris.

"It means that this is my last block week away, so it better be a good one."

"I am hoping for London, plenty to do down there, enough nightlife, clubs, the lot." Said Sandra.

"Can I have everybody's attention, please? This year for the block week we will stay in Scarborough on the east coast. As you all know, this will be part of the 'Rural Economy' module and so we will study the economy of the Yorkshire Wolds."

The Professor received a few groans from the students.

"You will all look at how the local farms and agricultural industries are functioning. Are the farms diversifying? Are the changes ensuring the future of jobs and economic activity? What sort of jobs are located there? This is an important part of the course."

"What week will that be, sir?" Asked Aze.

"The week of March 23rd."

"March 23rd! The cricket world cup, I can't miss that!"

"Yes, well, we will all be leaving on the 23rd. The pickup will be at the front of this building at nine am. Nine am sharp. Any more questions?"

"Will we need hiking gear?" Asked Sandra.

"Great question, yes, we will step out into the countryside there so bring along some proper attire, waterproof clothing and walking boots."

"Scarborough, the jewel of the east coast." Said Chris.

"I live just down the road from Scarborough. It is not a gem; I am not thrilled about it. There is nothing going on in Scarborough in March apart from the old geezers shuffling about on the promenade." Said Sandra.

"Who cares about that, it is the cricket world cup in Australia, and I am going to miss it!" Said Aze.

"I bet it will freeze in March, on that coast. Hope we get a decent place to stay." Said Jack.

"We will make something happen." Said Chris. Attempting to secure a bit of excitement.

"Yeah, that place will blow up." Said Bob.

Disappointed, the students left with the news and continued with their day.

30
PREPARATION

The few weeks up to the weekend before the block week departure came and went without incident. On Sunday evening Jack packed for the upcoming five days in Scarborough, a small suitcase and backpack. His mind was not on the trip but more directed at what his choices would be after. His relationship with Angie had moved, so that they were now seeing each other on a regular basis. After her win with the big horse racing bet, she had left her job and was now thinking of her next step. She had always dreamed of getting a boat and sailing away. Maybe Jack would come with her? For the next week, Angie would come over and stay at Jack's caring for Snoop and the house while he was away on the rural study. Jack hoped she would decide to stay longer, much longer. Angie was determined to do just that.

Work was weird and Jack was struggling to focus on his job. The dark cloud hanging over everyone's head muted the energy and it was just not the same place. The only chatter at the drinks machine was about budget cuts and job losses. His work would consider his position and funding after he returned in a week. All Jack wanted was something positive to look forward to. His hope was on Angie. The worry over work could wait.

His cell phone vibrated in his pocket, Jack pulled it out and answered. It was Crumb.

"Hey, how are you doing?"

"Are you free on Wednesday night?" Said Crumb.

"No, I will be away, with my course. Why?"

"We have another gig set up. We need a driver."

"Just cannot do it, Crumb. Can you leave it for another week? I might need some work, depending on what they are doing with my job."

"No, it is urgent, we have information on a delivery that will come in and we have a buyer set up and waiting."

"Not fireworks, I hope!"

"No, sausages this time."

"Bangers then."

"Hilarious. Aren't you?"

"Anyway. I'm Sorry, I just can't do it. Keep me in mind if you have anything after next week. I might have nothing else to do."

"You are our number one, you know that."

"Yes, I know. I will see you when I get back, next weekend."

The call ended and Jack texted Angie.

'Hey, you OK to come over tonight x?'

'Sure, just finishing up my packing.'

'Cool, I'm doing the same, nearly done.'

'I'll be over in an hour, x.'

31
KEN

onday, the first day of the block week, the journey to get there. The Entrance lobby at the university held the students as they gathered to wait for their transportation. They milled around cases and bags piled against the lobby walls. Professor Tresswell paced along the front of the building; his scuffed brown brogues squeaked in alternating notes as he walked.

On schedule and as planned, a white Scania series coach approached the front entrance and stopped, its air brakes hissed. The company had branded the coach with black outline gold lettering as the 'Ken Mold Executive Coach'. The vehicle sat at the entrance to the university for a moment before its door opened. Professor Tresswell approached and set his right foot on the bottom step of the doorway into the bus. As he leaned in, a pungent, thick aroma met his sensitive nose as he took a breath. He coughed.

"Hello." Said Tresswell, he noted the driver seemed distracted and restless, and rather uncomfortable in his seat.

"Scarborough?"

"Are you picking up?"

"Oh, aye, Prof, I'm Ken. You are the Prof, I presume? The week in Scarborough?" Said Ken as he came out of his trance and stopped squirming in his chair.

"Yes, good and early I see. Can we load them up?" Asked Tresswell.

"Yep, let us get them all on. The sooner we get going, the better. I must make a stop or two on the way, a dose of a tummy issue. It's stirring a bit; can you hear it?"

Ken lifted his shirt with his right hand and placed the bus microphone onto his bare stomach with the other. The microphone was cold, he shivered but persevered. He pressed hard to get the best contact with his distended belly. Then, amplified through the sound system, a substantial, bubbly growl echoed throughout the bus and onto the street beside it. Passersby could hear the noise and hastened on without stopping or looking back. A pressurized geyser overdue for release. It sounded very dangerous, a character from a sci-fi movie. Nobody wanted to be around that.

"Oh, yes, there it is, not long now, mate." Said Ken, his brough furrowed like a ploughed potato field, his left eye watered as he spoke.

In a hurry, and with a concerned look, Tresswell turned to the students, who by this stage had formed a line to board the coach.

"This is it, the bus, please hurry, everybody on, please hurry."

"Here we all are then. I am Ken your driver of Ken Mold Executive Coaches. Your owner, manager, and driver. Good to see you all and welcome onboard. As you can see, it is an executive with all the facilities at the back. I should mention, though, that if I were you, I would not use the on-board bathroom for a few minutes, if you know what I mean."

Yes, the students understood very well. There was no mistaking it; the aroma emanating from the closed restroom door told the tale.

"I had a nice curry last night and er, well, it is passing right through me like a train of Afghans through the Khyber Pass."

With no hesitation, Ken placed the mic on his stomach again, He wanted to get another validating sound effect. He did and it left the passengers in no doubt.

"Monster from the deep, eh? Oh, there she blows."

"So, we'll be taking the M18, stopping at the first available services, and I'll be the first out or we are all in trouble."

The bus door closed, the students captured, desperate to redirect the ventilation system, and the coach departed. It sped to its destination, several unscheduled stops away.

32
HOTEL

Before the age of unbridled, unedited, and sometimes cruel, online hotel reviews, we would obtain consideration of the quality of a hotel from word of mouth or a visit to a travel agency. The details of a stay having regard to the accommodation at the destination. The Great Eastern Hotel did not depend on obtaining business from such review, or gossip, as its management opined, it managed just fine, with or without guests. And it did so all year round.

The Great Eastern Hotel faced the sea and took in the ocean air on the east coast of England, in Scarborough. The town was renowned by tourists as a bustling summer destination. But on a crisp March evening it was a very different place. Deserted streets, closed shutters, empty beds, and vacant rooms. The bulk of tourists would not be back for at least two months. That was undeniable.

At four-stories in height, the converted Victorian stone terrace was a handsome structure. The front of the building was complete with original bay windows and a gray slate roof. Together, these elements provided an elegant, detailed facade for the hotel. The main floors stood over a basement which, because of its height, raised the ground floor above street level. Thus, to access the entrance visitors used eleven well-worn steps. The wear evidenced the many patrons who had frequented the building over the years. The hotel lobby and reception area lay beyond.

At the top of the steps, beside the entrance door, sat a black cat. A scraggy and bedraggled animal. She was relishing the sun and taking whatever warmth it could lend beside a large full leafed cardoon pot plant. The foliage of the plant twisted as the breeze picked up strength from the east and brought with it a choppy edge to the sea.

The entrance door to the hotel opened. Part by part, the hotel chef emerged onto the highest step. First a foot, a leg, the right arm, and the rest followed, only, it seemed, by attachment. It was a simple task to observe his occupation by his hat, a toque. A tall white cap used by this profession that sat upright on his head. The cat paid little regard and did not move.

The chef stood for a moment, an unshaven man in his forties. His clean starched hat was a contrast to his creased blood splattered apron. He removed the toque with one hand, a volume of oiled hair tumbled onto his forehead. A shake of the head and a flailing sweep of the free hand returned the hair into its position. He locked it away in a flash, captured under the rim of the hat.

"Skitt!" Said the Chef.

Ken now appeared much better. The second half of the drive had been much smoother, and the air in the coach had greater freshness. He swung the coach onto the street in front of the hotel.

The chef with minimal movement glanced sideways, first at the bus and later at the cat. In an instant he snatched the cat under one of his arms, with the other he grasped a handful of leaves and stems from the pot plant. With both in hand, he darted back into the hotel at a pace three times that at which he emerged. The entrance door swung to a close with a loud creak.

The 'KEN MOLD EXECUTIVE COACH' halted at the entrance to the hotel. Ken picked up the mic and announced.

"Here we are then, all out, I'll be staying at a different place in town. I got myself a decent room to bunk at this week, instead of using the bus."

He peered at the hotel with his familiar grimace.

"All-inclusive, you know. If any of you ladies' care for a curry and a drink, let me know, I've got a double and I'm feeling much better now, plenty of room."

He followed his remark with a wink of his eye as he opened the coach door by pushing the small button on his right side. The students, carrying backpacks and various items of luggage, emerged from the bus one-by-one and made their way up the steps into the hotel lobby. Ken observed them as they disembarked and drove off the instant everyone was off the coach. Accompanied by the sound of Dixie playing on the air-horns as the bus departed, Tresswell jumped.

33
ELBOW

Overwhelmed by its new guests, the compact rectangular space of the entrance and lobby of the Great Eastern Hotel bulged at its seams. The group followed the track worn into the nylon weave of the carpet, which led from the entrance door to the reception desk. The desk, an homage to the seventies, a thick marble countertop supported by a back-lit dark paneled wood plinth. In a moment, they would hide the carpet from view as the tidal swell of student bodies compressed within the confines, filling it to more than capacity. Tresswell, windmilling his arms in a sort of butterfly swimming motion, made his way through the mass to the small desk and the receptionist behind. Jack took some time and stood at the periphery of the crush to consider a sign just inside the entrance door. The notice seemed to have been constructed either in haste or without care, blue pen, ink smudged by the writer, on a sheet of crumpled white paper, the sign read:

'WELCOME TO THE GREAT EASTERN HOTEL.'

'DINNER SERVED AT 6:30 p.m.'

'Chef's Dinner Special.'

'Braised Rabbit Pie served with Seasonal Greens.'

Jack was considering the menu when he received an elbow in his side, just above his right kidney, harder than he would expect from one of his fellows. He winced and let out a gasp.

"Excuse me, thank you." Said a tall, well dressed older man as he emerged from the huddle of students pressing against the reception desk like a cork leaving a bottle of cheap bubbly. He turned towards a room that had a sign above its door, 'DECK'. Jack supposed that the room was the dining room.

"Sorry." Said Jack as the man wandered on and said no more.

Amongst the seething throng of students, Tresswell, having spoken to the receptionist, turned, waved a large wooden key fob, and said:

"We will need to have two to each room, you all need to decide who goes where. I am off to my room, the 'LOBSTER' on the top floor, so I will see you all tomorrow for our first outing."

"With me, Russ?" said Jack. Pulling at the elbow of Russ' jacket.

"Where?"

"Sharing a room?"

"Sharing? Hm, yeah, yeah, that would be fine. You arrange it, please."

While the others in the group discussed their room sharing arrangements, Jack made his way through to the reception desk and gained the attention of the receptionist. She was a well-dressed, petite woman in her late thirties. Her name tag identified her as Katherine. The receptionist peered upwards over the top of the counter.

"Hello, Mr.?" Asked the receptionist.

"Hello, Katherine. yes Headland, Mr. Headland." Said Jack.

"OK, Mr. Headland. You will be in room two, twin beds, on-suite. Who are you sharing with?"

"That will be Russ Blower."

Jack turned and pointed to a distracted and nervous Russ as he scanned around the lobby. Russ had observed that the door marked 'KITCHEN STAFF ONLY' was ajar. And, on closer inspection, had seen the glassy reflection of an eye as someone peered through the small gap between the door and its frame.

"OK. The room is at the end of that corridor to the left. Here are your entry keys."

The receptionist pointed towards the corridor to the left of the lobby area and handed Jack two sets of room keys. Each a large wooden fob three times larger than the key itself and marked with a '2' and the words 'HERMIT CRAB' inscribed. As he turned, Jack saw the chef as he appeared from behind the door surveyed by Russ. The chef charged with a tipped toed series of steps down the corridor into a door marked 'CELLAR.' He carried with him a limp bundle under his left arm.

"Crikey, he's in a hurry!" Said Jack.

"I don't like the look of that." Said Russ, as he shifted his position to hide behind Jack.

"Nobody should trouble you in here, nothing to fret about, I am certain. Your group is the only one in the hotel this week. So, it should be quiet. We serve meals in the Deck dining room, which is right behind you. Dinner is at six thirty in the evening. Breakfast buffet, continental style, starts at six each morning. We hope you have a great stay. Anything else I can help you with?" said Katherine, from behind the desk.

"Thank you no, that's all good." said Jack.

Jack felt another elbow jab in his ribs, this time less painful. He turned, half expecting to see the tall man again, but instead it was Aze.

"Hey Jack, would ya?" Said Aze as he nodded in the receptionist's direction.

"Would ya?"

"Yes, would ya? You know the receptionist?"

"Not now, Aze."

Jack ignored Aze and turned to Russ. He handed him a set of room keys. Russ examined one key by running his finger down the serrated edge.

"I am not confident that the locks to these keys will be strong enough to keep anyone out. I will need to make sure that the doors are secure."

"OK, Russ, here we go, the room is going to be down there on the left."

"Get to the room, quick."

Jack and Russ gather their cases and backpacks and head towards the corridor.

"Did you notice that old guy in the lobby, he was looking at us? And that Chef, the one with the hat, did you see him? He ran down to the cellar. I dislike the feel of this place. Some funny things going on here. I am keeping myself to myself this week." Said Russ.

"Never mind all that, come on Russ. It will be fine."

34
CRABS

O therwise known as the Hermit Crab, room 2 the only door at the end of a shadow filled corridor, a few steps away from the lobby and reception area. Russ rushed ahead and unlocked the door with some urgency to enter first. He looked around. The room was an interior room with no windows. The decoration old but clean. Two bedside tables, a modest wardrobe, a desk, chair, and a set of small drawers made up the furniture. A door on the left-hand side of the room led to the bathroom and shower. The hotel had composed the interior design of the room on a crustacean theme, with framed paintings of various crabs hung on the walls. Jack imagined the other rooms would have similar themes and wall hangings, perhaps lobsters, shrimps, barnacles, and seabirds.

"Is it OK if I take the bed that is the furthest from the door?" Said Russ as he sat on the bed furthest from the door.

"Yeah, no problem. This one works for me; I can be next to the door, no problem." Said Jack as he placed his backpack and case on the bed that remained.

"I just don't trust the people here. There is something about them. It does not feel right. Take my word, something is fishy here." Said Russ.

"And not just the decor? Well, we have seen little of them yet, but I do not think they mean any harm. The receptionist was genuine enough. You just need to settle in and get on with it."

"Well, I'm not taking any risks. I have my personal alarm. It is going under my pillow tonight."

Concerned so much about potential intruders, Russ pulled the chair from under the desk and toward the door. He then lent it at forty-five degrees, so its top wedged against the door to prevent it opening without effort. In addition, he bolted the door, checked that it was secure, tugged at it with some force, and undertook this sequence twice over.

"That should keep them out."

"I don't think there's any issue, but OK, there you go, hope it satisfies you that will keep them out."

"You will thank me, you will see. Anyway, my wife packed up some goodies just in case the food here is not appealing."

Russ opened his bag and removed a bag of sweets, candy, biscuits, and other small snacks. He heaped them together on the table closest to the door, next to Jack's bed.

"Help yourself, there's plenty where those came from. My wife's good to me, she loves my smooth arms, you know."

As he spoke, Russ rolled his shirtsleeve up to his elbow and exposed his forearm. He pointed his arm toward Jack as he rubbed it up and down with the palm of his other hand. Disturbed, Jack felt uncomfortable and backed away.

"Nice and smooth. Here you go have a feel."

"That is fine Russ, I'm sure your wife wouldn't want me messing around with your arms. So, I am OK. I am very OK. If you do not mind, I will use the shower first, while you are unpacking. Then we should get dinner. We have got forty-five minutes."

"I might have an early night. Don't know if I can face the staff here." Said Russ, his instinct informed him that something was awry.

"Do not lock me out with that chair if you stay in."

The Deck was a large room converted from at least two smaller rooms on one floor. It had an area large enough to fit ten or more circular dining tables with ease. The staff had laid each table with serving and eating utensils and various dinner service items. Framed drawings of local wildlife adorned the walls, rabbit, seagull, cormorant, shag, and more. The tall man occupied a table at the window, alone. He gazed with an intense stare at anyone who entered the room. It was six-thirty and members of the student group filtered in and took seats at various tables.

"Over here." Said Bob. He gestured to Jack and Chris to join him.

"What is going on?" Said Jack.

"Nothing much."

"Hiya, boys. I like the décor, very David Attenborough, don't you think?" Said Chris.

"Yes, very. Enough of the sarcasm." Said Jack.

"Well, I'm right, aren't I?"

"Suppose it's better than nothing."

"Who's being sarcastic now?"

"Where's Aze at?" Said Bob.

"In the 'Mollusk room' he has a TV, and it's tuned to cricket. He is watching that with interest. Pakistan are playing Australia." Said Chris.

"Let us get out of here and explore this town. There must be a local pub close by. We have the first field trip tomorrow and Tresswell will play a blinder, you will see." Said Bob.

The others agreed, and they departed from the Deck under the watchful eye of the tall man.

35
CELLAR

The cellar, accessed from the lobby by thirteen worn carpeted steps, was out of bounds to hotel guests. That by itself caused no alarm, and nor should it. But the schemes and projects that unfolded within that basement room were another tale. Those enterprises were not new, they had taken place for several years and they had become more intense over the last few months. The hotel operated above not because of them but as a cloak to them. Guests, untouched by the industry below, went about their everyday lives, oblivious.

The chef peered through a narrow opening between the kitchen door and its jamb into the lobby. He needed to get to the cellar before it was time to prepare dinner. The area was at capacity with the new student guests as they bustled amongst themselves at the hotel reception desk. There was a clear path to the cellar door behind them. He could make it with none of them noticing if he were quick enough. Under his left arm a bundle, swathed in a thick cotton tea towel, limp at both ends.

When the moment arose, he dashed from the kitchen to the closed cellar door and opened it. Nobody had seen him, he thought. The steps to the cellar were steep. A single exposed bulb attached to a thin wire hung from the ceiling half-way down the passage and provided enough light. He held onto the bannister and hurried to the locked door at the foot of the passage. The door was solid save two small rectangular glazed transom window openings above its frame. A warm amber glow spread into the small footwell at the foot of the stairs from the openings. He knocked on the secured door with the back of his right hand, with an arrangement of spaced and timed raps.

"Who is that?" Said a muffled voice from behind the door.

"Pit." Said the chef. He glanced up the stairs and established that no one had followed.

Now unbolted Pit opened the door. The room was an almost perfect square and lit with a soft light. Inside stood Peet, who was Pit's brother, and who also worked at the hotel as a server. When stood together, despite their two-year age difference, it was difficult to take them apart. It was only because Pit always wore his torque that you could do so. Also, in the room was an older woman, a regular visitor they both knew, but her name they did not, as she never revealed it. They knew her as the accountant. Pit entered the cellar and closed the door behind him. They all stood together beside a small table in the center of the room, there were no chairs. Pit removed the bundle from under his arm, laid it on the table and unfurled the tea towel. Inside was a taped parcel, about the size of a couple of clay house bricks laid end to end.

"Ricky dropped this today. There will be much more on Thursday."

"That looks like thirty thousand." Said Peet.

"Just about. We will learn for sure when we count it, put it in the machine." Said Pit.

The accountant was silent as Peet unwrapped the parcel and gathered up the two piles of bank notes it contained. He collated them into a single stack the same height as the bear bottle that Peet had placed on the table. He held it with both hands. In the far-left corner of the room was a banknote counting machine which could count up to a thousand notes per minute. By its side, on the wall, was a chalkboard that contained a series of numbers. They used the machine on a regular occasion. Sometimes the vibration of its work would carry through the structure to the dining room above, so their schedule was to avoid mealtimes. He placed the money into the feeder at the front of the machine. The equipment whirred for a few minutes while they all stood in silence, then Peet read from the counter.

"You were close. It is twenty-nine thousand and four hundred." Said Peet.

The accountant crossed the room to the chalkboard, stretched as high as she could, and noted the figure.

"Looks like we will have some accident this week, maybe a considerable water leak and room closure." She spoke with the certainty of a clairvoyant.

"We will need to establish how we will account for the delivery that is showing up later this week. If it is much more than what we have now, Ricky will demand to know how we will deal with it. I for one do not have a clue."

They stared at each other in silence. This was an unexplored issue. The value of cash arriving each week was escalating at a daunting pace. There was only so much loss that they could account for within the hotel business to cover the flow without raising suspicion. It would disappoint Ricky if they could not determine a suitable process to launder the money. They were all mindful that a disappointed Ricky would mean trouble, big trouble.

36
WOLDS

Today, Tuesday, the second day of the block week, was the day for the student outing into the countryside. The group had settled into their accommodation, had a good night's sleep, and enjoyed a continental breakfast. All apart from Russ, who was taking every and any precaution as the contents of his jacket pocket would tell. The tips of his fingers played at random as he alternated his grip on the objects it held; a rabbit's foot, a crucifix, a silver coin found on a beach and a dried acorn, they provided some comfort.

Kens' executive coach arrived at the hotel, and the group boarded without conversation of any substance. The weather being the chief topic. The overcast gray cloak hid any sign of the morning sun, keeping hope in its pocket. Ken was quiet. He read the itinerary for the day and shuffled in his seat, ready to take the group to their destiny. Tresswell peered over his glasses and looked at Ken with disguised apprehension, recalling the previous scenario. The Professor crossed the fingers of his left hand behind his back and prayed for St. Christopher to issue a calm digestive system to all in proximity. In a moment, they were out of town and cutting into the damp mist that hung over the landscape, consuming any hint of color that it may hold.

Their first destination, Sneaton Thorpe, a typical English Yorkshire Wolds village in sight of Whitby Cathedral to the east. Whitby lay on the same coast as Scarborough, but further north. Russ knew Whitby was famous as the setting and inspiration for Bram Stoker's "Dracula". This alone further convinced him he was in mortal danger. He grasped the rabbit's foot, tight, then searched for his lucky coin.

After twenty minutes of travel, the bus approached the village and the empty main street. Nestled together were a few stone-built houses and farm buildings ordered by the low stone walls that lined the street. The village centered on the Wilson Arms pub and St. Bridget's church and graveyard. As the bus slowed, Tresswell arose from his seat and pointed his finger to Ken to show the precise location to stop, it was beside the graveyard.

A beige colored safari suit set Tresswell ready for an expedition, however today he would not leave the confines of the bus. He picked up the mic from its place holder beside Ken and announced the itinerary for the study. The rustle of his beard, amplified as it pressed against the mic, muffled his first words.

"Attention everyone, we are here at our first study point. You all know that the aim of this study is to assess the traditional Wolds upland farming economy. And how it is being assisted by a growing number of home workers and rural businesses, both activities boosting local communities. The economic benefits of tourism help maintain the unique

Wolds character and environment, but is the economy sustainable?"

"I need a group of six." He said then sounding out the numbers one to six and pointing at random passengers. He chose Jack, Bob, Chris, Sandra, Jane, and Simon. As Tresswell turned to look at his student list, Aze, not part of the group, joined as they left the bus without notice.

Bob was the last one out. He stopped at the top of the steps and turned to Tresswell.

"When do we get picked up?"

"Not here. You will get picked up in Whitby, it's a two-mile walk from here. We will meet you at the Whitby quay parking area. Just follow the roadway signs and directions to town, we show it on the handout you have for today's activities. It should not take you over thirty minutes to get there. The bus will pick you all up at four-thirty. That gives you a few hours to investigate the village and to get some lunch. I expect an excellent report and full photographic record."

"OK Ken, away we go to the next village. Has anyone seen Aze?" Said Tresswell as he looked around the bus and checked his student list again.

"Right, off we go, colonel." Said Ken.

The door closed, Tresswell appeared puzzled, Ken sounded the horn in triumph. With no hesitation, the bus moved on to the melodic sound of Dixie as it woke the village from its slumber. The sky thrown full of circling birds as they left the comfort of their roosts. Russ' ghostly face pressed against the rear window as the bus left the graveyard behind. He gripped the crucifix in his pocket and gazed upwards at the church spire.

37
VILLAGE

The birds knew. They knew a herd of deer, a litter of puppies, a hive of bees. The collective murder of crows knew. An omen, a connection to superstition, a long-held belief that a sighting of these birds issued a portent of doom. The birds gathered in expectation that death would arrive as their companion close after.

Kens' executive coach left the village and withdrew through the mist into the distance, forming small spirals of swirling condensation held in midair by its wake. The group looked on with a certain desperation. The village was too still. By fate or omen, the murder of crows now circled above them and the spire of the church, the birds chattering among themselves. Apart from their incessant cackle, angry for being disturbed so early, there was no other sign of life. Jack half expected a tumbleweed, a loose bundle of vegetation, to carry down the empty street, like a scene from a classic western, the moment preceding a shootout.

St. Bridget's church supported a narrow dark spire on a stone tower and sat within the grounds of a small graveyard. The church lay in front of the group as they moved off the roadway. At the entrance to the churchyard, the village council had sited a blue plaque, a historic marker. The bright gold lettering on the panel outlined the church's history, so it was available to visitors to enjoy. Bob, being a visitor today, read it aloud.

"St Bridget's chapel held in the 12th century by the Arundels and descended with the manor until 1290. It was one of the chapels of Whitby granted to the abbey by the founder, an unrecorded benefactor. The church of St. Bridget reconstructed in 1823 by Henry Wilson of Sneaton Castle. It comprises a nave of four bays, a shallow sanctuary, south portico, and western tower. The tower at the west end has an octagonal lantern capped by a short pyramidal spire and contains three bells only accessible by ladder. On the south portico and also within the church are carvings of the Wilson coat of arms. There is some reason to assume that the latter form of adornment, of which there are several occurrences in the parish of Whitby, is a portrayal of St. Bridget's legacy. St. Bridget is the patron saint of Sweden, a mystic who had many revelations, some which she fulfilled, some which she did not."

The group surveyed the church, its gothic architecture commanded the property in which it sat. A mist continued to hold tight to the ground and swirled amongst and between the arrangement of gravestones in front of the chapel. A low dry-stone wall described the perimeter of the church grounds and held the mist in place. Large flat stones lay on top of one another, their weight enough to maintain their place; but now entangled with roots that intertwined and acted as strong as any mortar could. The wall had always been there, long before the church and any of its worshippers.

"Not much going on here." Said Jack. He bent his head backwards to gaze at the whirlpool of circling birds above, they squawked. "Apart from those vultures!"

"Think positive. In every village there is a tavern, a place that they will welcome us with open glass." Said Chris.

"And a graveyard. The dead center." Said Jane. She smirked and then dashed, camera in hand, towards the graveyard and a narrow opening in the wall, guarded by an ornamental wrought-iron gate. At the center of the gate, a rusted iron roundel of a bird in flight gave Jack a moment of déjà vu. Was that the emblem in his daydream? He shivered; the gate made a heavy, unoiled scrape as Jane pushed her way through it. Unenthused, the group followed. She held the gate open for them as they passed through one by one. In the cemetery, Jane photographed all that did not move, which was everything.

The gravestones were intricate, ornamental, and arranged in neat, ordered rows, but amongst them three stones stood different. The group wandered through the graves, careful to not step on them; they noted the inscriptions.

"If we log the names and dates, we can get a picture of the historical personality of the village." Said Jane as she continued to photograph. "But wait, they all have the same last name, 'Wilson', what do you see?"

"Not, these three, here." Said Jack. Bob joined him. "Decorated different and they appear to be more recent, not like the others. But they all date from the sixties."

Inscribed on the face of each of the stones were letters and dates; J. H 1946-1965, G. M 1943-1965, and E. H 1944-1965 on the center stone. The graves appeared to be well-tended and tidy and sat together under a large oak tree. A vase stood alone on the ground stone of the middle plot, in it was a fresh flower arrangement. In fact, it was the only grave that had fresh flowers in the whole yard.

"Super interesting. But I am done with this. I need a beer, or two, to better digest this incredible find." Said Chris, sauntering with little intent, scrubbing the soles of his shoes on the gravel path.

"Well, these do not have surnames, so I suppose they could still be Wilson's." Said Jack. "Something awful must have taken place in 1965. Don't you think?"

"Maybe the pub closed early? There must be a pub around here someplace. That is where the real rural economy is. And that is a fact." Said Chris. "I think it should be close to the church, so that locals could pray at the venue of their choice. In honor of the spirit in either case."

"It is too early for beer for me, but I wonder if they have the Cricket highlights on TV?" Said Aze.

"By the look of things, you'll be lucky if they have electricity. Anyway, how did you get off the bus right in front of the Prof?" Said Jack.

"Nimble is my middle name. That is how. Quick between the wickets. There was no way I was going to get lumbered with Russ and Tony."

The group left the graveyard using an alternative to the path they had first stepped on and turned left towards the center of the village. Across the street was a large stone and brick barn. It was the Whitby Rock warehouse. A large sign on the façade of the building described the use. The business had converted the handsome structure into a warehouse and shop. A small retail unit connected to the front of the building displayed an assortment of colorful Whitby Rock candy in the window that faced the street.

38
HELALDRY

A manageable walking distance beyond the warehouse and on the same side of the street as the graveyard was the Wilson Arms pub. Accommodated within an 18th Century building, the pub had an attractive historic front elevation, its exterior a lime plaster finished in white. A projecting sign hung above the entrance and made a grating squeak as it moved back and forth on its hinge. The sign bore the heraldic coat of arms of the Wilson family. The name came from a connection to Sir William de Waldershelf, who accompanied William the Conqueror during the Norman Conquest of England in 1066.

Jack noted the crest. What did the sign mean? A silver wolf, upright on its hind legs, set on a black background that carried three golden stars and a crescent moon circled by golden serpents. In heraldic terms, silver represented purity, gold denotes elevation of the mind, and black symbolizes grief. The crescent moon points to a connection to heaven, while the serpents embody sin. The stars a celestial goodness, while the wolf represented an honor given for hard industry. Jack knew very little of this, not sufficient to make any sense from it, if there was any to make. Maybe Robin would know.

"There's the pub, come on guys I've had enough of this rambling lark." Said Chris.

"My guess is that the pub is full of Wilsons, not long before the grave." Said Jack.

"That is not funny." Said Sandra, but she laughed anyway.

The interior of the pub was such like a typical English village pub, not changed for at least thirty years. The tables and chairs were all worn and unstable, marked with the history of nights of drinking and revelry. But you would not know that now. The front bar area was empty. Behind the counter, a door to a back room was ajar and the shadows of several figures played in the sliver of light seen through the gap. The sound of a whispered conversation heard, but they could not untangle the words.

"No-one here, they must all be out digging more graves." Said Chris.

"So long as they are not for us. Anyway, listen. They're speaking out the back there, it does not sound English, does it?" Responded Jane.

"Whatever language they use, I wish they would hurry, I'm perishing of thirst here, my throat is dry as a bone." Said Chris.

"Another reason the graveyard is full. Hey, Jack. Look, the cash register is just there. I could just hop over the bar, grab the cash, and make a run for it. In fact, I could grab the whole thing!"

"Wow. Big time move that, Chris, big time move." Said Jack.

"Why would you do that? Caught as soon as you left the pub, that's what would happen. Nowhere to go. Running around with a cash register! How much do you think is in there, anyhow? I bet there is a fifty quid float at the most. So how would you get away? You need to plan anything like that to even get away with it and have a 'Plan B' if it went wrong."

"It would be useful to pick up some extra cash, though." Said Chris.

"Yeah, maybe, but one big job would be better than fifty small ones. Less risk of being caught if you stuck at one if no-one got hurt and it was all planned out. A spur-of-the-moment job is not the way to go. Believe me, I know. You need the cash?"

"Don't we all? Here we go, here is the landlady."

A tall brunette woman in her mid-40s appeared from the back room, the landlady who ran the pub. Her shoulder length hair floated to a rest as she came to a stop at the bar. A look of surprise expressed itself on her made-up face and pencil thin eyebrows, but not by design. The number of people waiting at the bar was unusual for this time of day, and of more impact was that none of them were locals. She tapped her varnished red fingernails on the bar counter.

"Blimey, more in today than we have had all week. Let us get you all sorted, I'll take your orders here, sorry for the wait."

An elbow hit Jack right under his ribs. It was becoming a regular experience, but still one that took him by surprise. He gasped in shock rather than in pain.

"Hey Jack, would ya?" Asked Aze.

"Would ya what?" Replied Jack.

"You know, would ya?" Said Aze as he nodded in the landlady's direction.

"Not now, Aze."

"Get the drinks in Bob. Last in and…"

"We need to get over to that Whitby Rock shop after this." Interrupted Aze

"Can we at least sit down first?"

The crows had lost interest and returned to their work in a nearby beet field. The mist had lifted with the warmth of the day, although the hiding sun offered no additional brightness. Through the front window of the pub, Jack noticed two men loading merchandise from a small white van at the side of the Whitby Rock warehouse. He thought he had seen them somewhere before, but the van obscured them, and he could not get an unrestricted view. The group ordered their drinks and sat together to chat. They did so until it was time that they gathered their belongings and left the Wilson Arms. The next stop was a visit to the shop across the street.

They entered the shop. Various sizes of rock candy all ordered and arranged on shelving in front of a counter area welcomed them. There is no one behind the counter, deserted the shop offered its wares.

"What is it about this place? Nobody around. Anywhere." Said Jack.

"I am going to look in there to see if anyone is about." Said Bob. He made towards a door located to the right and behind the counter area and gave a couple of knocks. After receiving no response, he opened it. It was dark inside, and he could not make out much, but from what he saw it was something being grown in long beds filled with dirt.

"Anyone there? Wow, that stinks in here. Jeez, it smells like a nail salon." Bob called and remarked as he returned into the shop.

"I think we should pick up some of this rock candy as an example of what type of business they do here." Said Sandra.

"I could manage something sweet." Aze.

"Well, let us take a selection and leave some cash on the counter." Said Sandra.

"We should just fill our pockets, no one is about." Said Chris.

"No, come on Chris, let us do as Sandra suggests. We can leave behind some money as payment. OK?" Said Jack.

"OK. OK." Said Chris.

The group each selected a few of the rock candy products at random. As he moved towards the counter, Jack stepped on a small container, about the size of a shoe box. It squashed under his foot, he had not noticed that it was there. Jack grabbed the box and picked it up. Half a dozen wrapped; coin sized rock candy fell into his hand from a split in its side. He examined them, turning them in his palm. They were the thickness perfect for popping whole into the mouth. Banded with multi-colored outer edges, they had quadrants of red, yellow, green, and blue stripping on their circumference. The candy contained on its surface lettering that read 'WHITBY' on the top and 'ROCK' in its bottom, both curved around the inner edge. A small red heart shape marked the center.

"I will take a few of these, I think my nieces will like them." Said Jack.

Jack put the candy in his jacket pocket and then placed an estimated contribution of money on the countertop. Adding to the cash that the others had placed there.

"Yes, my daughter will like these triangle shapes if I get to see her next week." Said Chris.

Chris remained in the shop until all the others had left. The last one out. He glanced around, then picked the money from the counter and placed it in his pocket.

39
CORMORANT

Whitby Abbey sat on the horizon of the headland, a ghost of its past; the ruined outline elevated above all other features. A marker to the student's destination, just as sailors used the Abbey's ruins as a landmark to prevent them running aground and ending as lost souls on the rocks beneath.

The group of lost student souls had made the two-mile walk from Sneaton Thorpe to Whitby in complete silence. The air was bitterly cold and cut through their outer garments to chill them to the core. Marching on the walkers counted down the miles as they passed road signs on the route until they finally saw their destination.

The Whitby quay carpark was a barren piece of property, its entire expanse exposed and willing to accommodate wind and drizzle. Which was fortunate, as there was a plentiful supply of both commodities this evening.

Dispersed in the morning to disparate groups, now all the students reunited at the designated Whitby quay parking area. They waited for Ken's executive coach to pick them up; they were looking forward to the warmth that it would provide. The group huddled together like penguins to better protect themselves from the stiff wind heading inland off the water. The sun, hidden now by the clouds, was going down, taking the last of the half-light with it. Day was coming to a close, and the temperature was dropping fast, it would not be long before frost and ice would cover the parking area. The cold air held their breath in suspension, as a magician would hold dry ice, but maybe only for dramatic purpose only.

They stood close together and gazed out to sea with the blank stare of a shipwrecked sailor. At the edge of the quay, Jack stood closest to the seawall and drifted into a daze. Rainbow reflecting oil-stained sea water lapped at the concrete below as it had done for tens of years.

Set into the mooring area between tall dock pilings, a variety of boats bobbed back and forth, pulling on their anchor lines. The vessels silhouetted against the reflections eventually brought to the seawall by the lapping waves. A solitary black seabird circled in the distance with no need for a collective noun to describe it.

"Hm, what is that over there? That bird over there. I think that is a cormorant." Said Simon as he pointed to a bird hovering over a piling in the distance.

"Yes, a cormorant, or a shag. Although I have never seen a shag." Said Robin.

He pulled a pocket-sized book of sea birds and thumbed through to a specific page. With further information applicable to the debate, he explained aloud.

"The cormorant, Corvus Marinus, or Sea Raven. Is a grand and conspicuous waterbird. It has an almost primitive appearance with its long neck and short wings making it appear like a feathered dinosaur. Cormorants hold their wings out to dry. Regarded by some as ominous and rapacious. The Shag is a bird of the same species and often mistaken for a Cormorant, has a plume under its neck."

"I recognize a good Shag when I see one." Said Simon.

"I very much doubt that!" Said Sandra.

The bird, seemly with knowledge of being the center of attention, plonked itself on a piling in an ungraceful mount. It then spread its wings in an attempt to dry them in the now steady drizzle.

"Hmm. Cormorant. No plume. Stretching its wings. Looking for crabs." Said Robin. As he peered up from the book and gazed back out at the bird as it stretched its wings as wide as they could go.

"Yes, that would make sense, so a cormorant, not a shag with crabs. You do not want a Shag with crabs." Said Simon.

"Crabs." Said Robin.

"Cormorant or Shag." Said Simon.

Behind the group, a small white van with the logo "WHITBY ROCK" entered the parking area and halted at a boat dock. The two occupants of the van leapt out as soon as it had stopped and signaled to a yacht anchored in open water. As they did so a small rowboat, with two occupants departed from the yacht towards the dock, the oars striking the water with tremendous effort, creating loud and visible splashes.

"He is sitting on the piling now. From what I observe, he must be a Cormorant." Said Robin.

"Yes, a long-necked Cormorant."

"So, agreed, a Cormorant with a long neck."

Robin closed his book with a sense of achievement. He tucked it away into his pocket with the appropriate page earmarked and patted it down with gratitude.

After the short rowboat was tied to the dock, the two occupants stepped ashore and headed to the van on foot. They carried a single briefcase and were escorted by the van's occupants. The figure carrying the case had distinctive blond shoulder length hair.

"Hey Jack, look at that guy over there!" Exclaimed Jane.

"He looks like your Udde! He must be the real thing!"

Jane pointed in the direction of the four figures heading back to the van.

"Wow, he does. Nice hair though, all his I am presuming. That van. Look, it says Whitby Rock on the side, they are from the shop in Sneaton. I hope they found the money that we left." Said Jack.

"Hey, here is the bus!" Shouted Bob.

"About freaking time." Said Jack.

Ken threw himself at the steering wheel and swung the coach into the parking area. At the same time sounded the horn as he came to a halt, his trademark. The students had become accustomed to Ken's antics and the screeching of Dixie and did not react. Unlike the four making their way to the van who all stopped dead in their tracks for a moment to consider the disturbance, before continuing.

The group made their way to the bus and to the warmth that it would provide. They hoped that Ken had stayed away from the curry.

"All aboard then. What have you guys been up to?" Said Ken.

"Watching a Shag." Said Jane.

"I should have got here sooner, liked to have seen that. A live Shag, eh?"

Ken winked, Jane shook her head and sighed.

Jack made his way to a seat closest to the waterside and gazed out of the window. A silhouette of the yacht was broken by the illumination of the bow and its name "SVAMP HOG — LYSEKIL".

"What is all that about then?" Jack asked himself aloud, no-one else cared or took any account.

40
DECK

I n most instances, guests have observed that the quality of venue and of the food that it serves have improved over the years. Hotels have marketed their offers of culinary delights and created glamorous and exotic offerings set at attracting the highest caliber of customer. Guests now demand a level of quality and are attracted by it. However, where the primary business of a hotel has no relation to what it announces at the front door, it is possible that the food and service of such will be of a low standard and of doubtful edibility.

The Deck in its turn would not disappoint compliance with this qualification. The Deck was the dining room at the Great Eastern Hotel where the hotel guests receive breakfast and dinner, whether they want it, or not. Now it was 6:15 p.m. and hotel staff, returned from the cellar, prepared to dispense the menu. They set the tables for three courses, for some guests that would be three too many. It was apparent to many of the student group who kept a sense of smell, that they would not be in for a treat tonight.

The aroma of scorched vegetation of unknown origin, mixed with the sourness of ripe cheese hung in the air and stung the eye. Projecting a picture of what was in store, the students resigned themselves to attend, knowing that a night out on the town would follow this ordeal, and would wash away the contamination that was about to occur.

At one table, set for four only, sat Russ, Bob, Jack, and Chris. The table, like the others in the room, laid with a cream cloth that featured, in prominent locations, various stains gathered from previous outings. Each cloth had its own arrangement of marks and swirls configured in a unique pattern. As they daydreamed, the four each figured the stains for a form of psychological inkblot test. Russ saw a leaf; Bob saw a cat, Chris saw a knife, and Jack saw a face. They were not to know it, but they were all correct in their perception.

In the center of the table, arranged in no order, were salt and pepper pots, a single artificial flower in a vase and condiments in individual containers. Russ sat bolt upright, his eyes wide and a look of shock captured his face, and said, "Hey! Look at the server, he is just like the chef! Identical! Do you think they are twins?"

The others at the table turned and looked over their shoulders in the same direction to get a better view.

"Careful, don't let him notice you are watching. Trouble, that is what we have here. Trouble. There is something about the fact that there are two twins here, to me that is trouble." Said Russ as he let out a vibrato tremble from his throat, followed by a high-pitched whistle, coordinated to perfection with the same hand waving gesture that the chef had made as the coach arrived first at the hotel. Some basic reason, some instinct, petrified Russ about this man and his alleged twin.

"Russ, twins are not unusual, and there are two, normally, they are no more likely to be serial killers than anyone else in this room. I do not think they have any thought to cause you, or any of us, any trouble. But I must admit they both seem to have an eye on you!" Said Jack, winking to unsettle Russ further.

"OK, never mind all of this. What are you going for, Russ?" Asked Chris, attempting to pull Russ back to reality. "Here, you look at the menu. Concentrate on that."

Chris pushed the menu under the Russ' nose. Russ pondered the minimal selection and regretted the fact that he had attended dinner.

SOUP

CREAMY SWEDISH MEATBALL AND MUSHROOM

or

LEAFY VEGETABLE & SEAWEED MINESTRONE

MAIN COURSE

BRAISED RABBIT PIE served with LOCAL SEASONAL VEGETABLES

or

CHICKEN SURPRISE served with FRESH PICKED GREENS

SWEET

STICKY-STICKY PUDDING AND CUSTARD

or

PUDDING WITH RICE

or

A BOARD OF LOCAL CHEESE

"I think, I think, I will try the vegetable soup, the pie and the sticky-sticky." Said Russ, hesitating, after a moment of consideration.

Peet had returned from the cellar and was now attending the tables as a server. Without a sound, he strode over to stand behind Russ without him noticing. In silence, Peet drew closer, close enough to hear Russ and take his order as he spoke.

"So that is the leafy vegetable and seaweed soup, the braised rabbit pie, and the sticky-sticky pudding. The chef will love you they are all his favorites." Said Peet, Russ flinched, then shivered as though someone had walked across his grave. Jack, Bob, and Chris followed with their orders.

"Hey Jack, you looked a bit done when you got on the bus this afternoon, I have never seen you look like that before now." Said Chris.

"Those guys drove me insane with their blabbering about that bloody bird. Cormorant or Shag, Cormorant or Shag, that is all they were going on about. Not that important, was it? That and the fact that I will not finish the course if the budget cuts get passed next month. Maybe I will not even have a job if they appoint a new consultant to work on the new grant project. It has been on my mind."

"Crickey, yeah? But they know you are good, your work that is, don't they?

Whitby Rock | Kev Freeman

"That does not make any difference. Not at that place. Anyway, that consultant is a friend of the mayor."

"Wowza. What are you going to do?"

"I know a couple of guys who work their own thing, I might drive for them again, they will keep me busy until I figure something out. Anyway, I enjoy driving. How is your work going?

"Work is OK, you know. I am struggling with making maintenance payments for my kid, though. And I have missed a couple of mortgage payments. Been short on cash and a need to do something this month, I am desperate."

"That is why you were talking the way you were in the pub?"

"Yeah."

"That will not solve your problem if you get caught. What will that mean for your little girl?"

"She will be OK. I do not get to see her much anyway."

"You will get to see her a lot less if you do not think it through."

"Well, let me know if you ever figure out a big score."

Peet interrupted them as he returned to the table with the bowls of soup. Russ jolted in his seat as Peet leaned towards the table, too close for his comfort.

"Here you are Sir, your soup."

Russ flinched again. He threw his upper body to the right as the steaming bowl appeared over his left shoulder. Peet

◌⁂ 186 ⁂◌

stepped forward close to Russ' ear and whispered in a low gravel strewn voice.

"The soup is boiling tonight, Sir. Be very careful. Boiling hot."

Russ gripped his chair tight as though he was amid an execution and distanced himself as far away as he could from Peet. He returned to be upright as the soup sat in front of him, Peet moving around the table to serve the remaining bowls. Peet departed and his heart rate subsiding, Russ picked up a spoon and stirred the grey liquid in the bowl before him. He took a tentative sip. His expression, curled lips and exposed tongue followed by a cough that would remove any hairball revealed the taste. It was not good, not good at all.

After a moment Russ grabbed hold of the vase and took it from the center of the table. He pulled out the artificial daffodil and tossed it to one side. Then he checked the contents; it was empty, as he hoped. Then Russ, in one move, poured the contents of his soup bowl into the vase with such a precise skill that not a drop spilled. The soup almost filled the vase which Russ returned complete with flower to its original location beside the stain that resembled the cat, as if nothing had happened.

"What are you doing, Russ?" said Bob.

"I just cannot eat that. The chef is going to be angry and so will his twin; the hairs on the back of my arms are standing up. One of these guys will be after me, you'll see. There is only one thing for it, if I can't eat it then I have got to dispose of it out of sight."

He dealt with the following course in the same way. He pushed the pie filling into the salt and pepper pots until there was no remaining space available within them or any of the other tabletop containers. Russ now had a problem; his only available course of action would involve the empty pockets of his jacket and trousers.

"Russ, you can't hide all of it. Just leave it!" Said Chris.

"Too risky. Just watch, I have done this before. And quiet you will draw attention." Answered Russ.

"Maybe he can." Said Jack as Russ pushed, prodded, and squashed, various quantities of whatever was laid out in front of him, potato, carrot, rabbit, and some limp green leaf, into his clothing.

"Tell them I do not want the pudding, I'm off, see you after dinner."

Russ got up from the table. His trouser pockets bulged with pieces of pie filling and seasonal vegetables. They were steaming hot, and the vapor escaped in sporadic puffs like an Icelandic geyser. He headed out of the Deck, a slow staccato walk. the apparent victim of some obscure congenital disease. No-one else in the restaurant noticed.

41
INGEST

The body breaks food down into its many constituent parts to extract what it needs and sometimes what it does not. Protein broken into amino acids. Starch broken into sugars. Fat, broken into namesake acids. The digestive system sorts, absorbs and transmits compounds to the serotonin receptors in the brain to provide a sense of satisfaction. However, the components of the meal served by the hotel may have lacked enough substance to satisfy the hunger of all who had attempted to partake of its delights.

Tony left the Deck soon after Russ and was still hungry. He could not think of anything else. Unsatisfied with the quality and quantity of the meal, he needed more. He had heard that Russ had a stash of candy and snacks in his room and hoped that some were still available. Tony was tall, at least a head over anyone else in the group, and it only took him a few long strides to make his way through reception and down the corridor to room number two. He neared the door and knocked; it was unlocked. In his hurry to return to the room, Russ had not installed his security system. The act of his knocking forced the door to open, just enough that a gap allowed him to poke his head through to get a view inside the room. It was empty.

As he pushed the door open, it found the back of the chair that Russ would position behind it to prevent unauthorized entry. Tony had to use more effort to move the chair and attached door across the carpet to open enough gap to get his body through to enter the room.

"Hello, Russ? Anyone here? Russ?" Called Tony as he entered the room.

He could hear Russ' voice, a song falling from the bathroom. He noticed the stack of snacks piled on the side table. Tony felt the bathroom door with his hand and pressed his ear against the surface. From within he could make out Russ singing a rendition of a familiar song from a musical that he could not place.

"Hey, Russ? Russ, are you in there? Russ?"

"Who is that? How, how, how did you get in?" Said Russ. Inside the steam of the bathroom. Reflected in a hand cleared circle of steamed mirror, a face complete with a lime green cosmetic facemask. His left arm, extended to its full, covered with white foam from the elbow to the wrist. He was shaving the arm with long, meticulous strokes of the razor. He hesitated as he heard the voice.

"Russ, it is me. It is Tony. The door was open. I knocked, I could hear that you were in here, so I came in."

"I was sure that I had closed the door! What if that chef guy got in, or his twin? It is a nightmare! I could be in danger, you know! They are scary guys."

Russ made a loud warbling whistling sound.

"Hey Russ, I'm sorry. The door was open and yes, I know you don't trust the chef or the other guy, but I am starving. I heard you had a few snacks to spare. Can I take a couple? I see them here."

"OK, OK, just make sure you shut the door, so it locks on your way out. Please. That chef will be in here like a flash if he gets the opportunity."

"OK, if you say so. Alright. Thanks anyway, Russ. I will close the door on my way out. Are you thinking of coming out with us all tonight?"

"I am uncertain, I will see how I am feeling, and I have got to clean out my pockets."

"All right then, I'll just grab a couple of snacks and I will be out of here."

Tony turned away from the bathroom door and headed over to the side table that just about held the pyramid stack of snacks. He grabbed as many as he could fit into his hand. A full assortment. He stuffed the lot into his largest jacket pocket. They would last him on his night out. Tony exited the room, relieved that Russ was still in the bathroom. He made sure that he pulled the room door shut behind him.

As soon as he was into the corridor, he pulled one snack from his pocket. At random, he picked out the Whitby Rock sample. He opened his hand, looked at the candy and read the lettering.

"Hmm, Whitby Rock."

He popped the candy piece into his mouth and grimaced once he tasted how very sweet the candy was. "Lots of sugar then!" Tony said to himself just as Chris walked into reception.

"Hey Tony, are you coming out with us in tonight? We are heading into town." Asked Chris.

"Sure, I will meet you down here in ten minutes. Just got to get my wallet from the room."

"OK, I am just looking for Aze."

"Not seen him. Just the rainbow. Can you see that?" Said Tony.

42
WEIRD

P rior to the hotel dinner, the student group had discussed a plan to hit the town for a night out. An expedition further into a discovery of the area's pubs and clubs. Even though it was out of season, there must be venues that would offer a flavor of the local nightlife. They were unaware that most of the local nightlife, knowing what lay in store, had ventured to a different town.

They assembled in the hotel lobby area, Jack, Bob, Chris, Tony, Sandra, Simon, and Jane.

"I know Russ is not coming along, but has anyone seen Aze?" Said Jack.

"Tuned into the cricket again. That is where he is; Sri Lanka is playing Kenya. Riveting." Replied Chris.

"Well then, we had better get off, it is almost eight o'clock."

"Come on, I am feeling good tonight!" Said Tony, as he danced around the others, his hands in the air.

"Calm down, Tony, we have plenty of time." Said Bob.

"Is he OK?" Asked Jack.

"He is hyper-active tonight; it must be the sea air."

"Or the food's given him the runs."

The seven students left the hotel and headed for town; they were looking forward to being able to forget about their studies for one night. After several hours they had done that, and they stumbled back into the lobby of the hotel one at a time. Chris was the first one to return and slumped into a chair in front of the unmanned reception desk. He looked up at the hands of the lobby clock on the wall opposite. It was 2:30 a.m. Jack was the next through the door.

"I am done, that was crazy." Chris said.

"I still might have crazy. I have got to get back in the room now, it is like Fort Knox in there. Russ will not be in the best of moods if I wake him up, this late. He says that he needs at least nine hours of sleep a night."

Bob, the next to arrive at the lobby. The door swung behind him with a loud sustained creek.

"Bob, where is Tony? I have not seen him since he got up onto the pool table in that last place and started throwing the balls through the windows. I thought he got away with you?" Asked Jack.

"He did. He is crawling up the street on all fours right now, like he his climbing Everest. There may be a wait before he gets here."

"He is OK though?"

"Been weird all night. Not himself, he was talking gibberish and wanting to fight everyone he met. He was acting mad. I saw Jane, Simon and Sandra get a taxi just before the pool table incident. I cannot blame them. They must be back here by now."

Tony appeared outside the hotel entrance doorway, having crawled up the steps. He pawed with both hands at the glass panel in the door, his face magnified like a fish in a bowl through a distortion in the pane. He blew hard and gulped for air before he pushed the door open. The others looked on and awaited the drama to come.

Tony crawled through the door, still on all fours. His knees transferred a charge of static electricity from his trousers as they scraped along the nylon carpet. His hair received the electricity like a Van de Graaf generator. Tony stopped, rolled over on his back like a stranded beetle, his hair now splayed in all directions like a mad scientist, legs and arms flailing around. He did not know up from down. Bob ignored his own safety and worked his way through the melee of flying limbs to help Tony to his feet. Tony now upright calmed into a trance. Eyes, disassociated from each other, danced around their sockets, wide and glazed, unable to still themselves for a moment of focus.

"Are you OK with him, Bob?" Said Jack.

"Yes, now he is on his feet. He will be OK. Come on Tony, let us get you back to our room."

Tony responded with a grunt and a gurgle of unknown origin or meaning. They dispersed to their respective rooms. Bob hauled Tony away, stumbling. Jack made his way back to his room and its secured door. The bed was only a few steps away, and he knew it would be difficult for him not to disturb Russ. A single click and the door unlocked; Jack entered the darkness of the room.

For a moment, as the door opened, a shard of light from the corridor lit up Russ' face as he slept, his hair covered by a net to protect what remained of his curls. Jack nudged and pushed the chair enough to gain entrance. The heavy brushing noise against the carpet did not cause any disturbance. Russ remained asleep. Once in, Jack closed the door, locked it, and returned the chair to its place with its back wedged against the underside of the door handle.

"Balloons inside a velvet hat, rabbits sliding on a sponge hill."

Jack stopped dead in his steps and slowed his breath. Russ talked and talked in his sleep. He had shared a room with Russ on previous occasions and had gotten used to the random phrases he uttered with no meaning. At first Jack had found it disturbing, there was no respite or cure, but now he knew and was almost accustomed to it, almost. The jumble of mixed-up nonsense gave Jack confidence that Russ was still asleep. Tired, he got into his own bed, pulled up the blankets and was soon asleep himself. Some time passed; he could not say how long as he had drifted into sleep.

43
PLANT

Awoken by a loud knocking at the door, Jack sat up in his bed. Dazed, he was uncertain where he was. The knock was there again, loud; it grew insistent. Now Jack was awake. Russ murmured.

"There is an ice cream at the door. It has a face on it. Chocolate. Ice, ice, wavey."

He was still asleep and remained so as the knocking on the door persisted, getting louder and heavier. Jack threw his blankets back and got out of bed. He stumbled towards the door. He avoided the room defense system with some skill and withdrew the chair so he could open it.

"Hang on." Said Jack in a whisper.

Jack opened the door a few inches, enough to peer out. The blue of his right eye and a stripe of his face illuminated by a sliver of light from the corridor as it broke into the room. Tony stood still as a mannequin on the other side. His expression was not his, wide-eyed and in shock. Dressed only in his underwear. His limp arms draped like ribbons at his side, the remains of a large, leafy potted plant sat on his head. The organic material balanced it seemed by a single root that ran down Tony's nose and dangled from its tip. The root moved back and forth, pointing in Jack's direction as he breathed.

"They have got him!" Tony shouted. Desperate with fear, genuine fear. His eyes darted and widened in time to his words.

"What is going on, Tony? What are you talking about?" Jack glanced at his wristwatch and pressed the button on its side to illuminate the digital display. The red led strip flickered and informed him of the time, 03:56.

"You know it is four o'clock! Who has got who? Is this real? It feels like I am in one of Russ's waking dreams!" Said Jack. Still dazed, he searched for an explanation. There was none he could reason, as Tony continued.

"Come quick, get him out of there! You can hear the machine!" Said Tony, before he turned and ran down the corridor and out of view. Jack sighed. He knew he had to follow. He turned to grab some jeans and a shirt.

"Please do not let the nose melt, hold it on there, it's dripping." Said Russ, as he continued to sleep talk. Jack left the room to search for Tony, closing the door behind him. Russ would never know and slept on, talking.

The corridor was quiet, and Jack headed toward the reception and lobby area. As he passed the kitchen, he saw Tony standing at the open cellar door. The light from the stairwell up lighted Tony's face and the plant on his head. It leant to one side like a beret.

Tony, with his right arm outstretched, as though he had seen a body snatcher, pointed down the stairway with his extended index finger. Jack stood beside him and peered down the stairs and towards the hallway and the door at its bottom. A hint of pale-yellow light flickered around its edge and through the two glazed panels at its top, disturbed by shadows of activity behind. There was movement within the cellar, maybe one figure, or more. The low hum of machinery made the hairs on the back of their necks stand and prickle.

"He is down there!" Said Tony. Whatever he thought was going on terrified him. The plant and its dangling root shook.

"The chef has got Bob! They took him. And they are doing things to him!"

"They have Bob. What do you mean? What sort of things?" Said Jack.

"Things. The machine! The machine is stretching him! Go help him!"

Jack knew that the only way to calm Tony down was to head down the stairway towards the cellar and whatever activity was going on in there. He descended and reached halfway to be directly under the single lamp that now hung above his head. The shadows behind the door moved. He could hear the rattling of a machine and conversation.

"What is going on?"

Jack heard a voice from the top of the stairs. He turned to look back over his shoulder.

"Bob!"

"Tony thinks you are down here!" Said Jack.

"Of course not. I am OK, what are you going on about? It is all OK. He got up out of the room and I've been trying to find him."

Jack returned to the top of the stairway and closed the cellar door. Tony now distraught, the plant fell from his head, and in its place remained a golf ball sized pyramidal shaped pile of dirt.

"What have I done? What have I done?" Realizing where he was and what he had caused hit Tony as he regained a semblance of reality.

"Come on, Tony, let us get back to the room." Said Bob.

"Is he going to be OK? He's been acting weird all night?" Asked Jack.

"Yeah, I have got him, you go back to bed. I will take care of him."

Bob held Tony by his elbow and guided him toward their room. Jack picked up the remains of the plant and dropped it into a nearby waste bin. He noted that a handful of its leaves were missing.

The hum of the machine in the cellar continued without further disturbance or concern.

44
STRANGER

Plans emerge, and schemes grow through chance meetings and serendipitous conversation. When the door of opportunity opens, it is a choice whether we enter or pass by. A stranger may sometimes bear such an opportunity. An attractive opportunity attached to past deeds the privilege which we are not likely to know.

Wednesday morning, the hotel had cleared the dinner service and remnants of food from various hiding places and made the Deck ready for breakfast. Now the room was bright and well illuminated, fresh tablecloths adorned the rearranged tables. Set out in regimental form, close to the kitchen entrance, a mix of continental style and traditional English breakfast food offerings. Food items, a compendium of coffee, tea, juice, toast, pastries, cereal, and fruits together with greasy, over-cooked sausage, bacon, and hard fried eggs. Peet managed breakfast. His task this morning was to ensure the food was stocked as guests passed through. He was the only staff member required to tend to the few trays, as guests would help themselves to the fare.

Bob was the first of the student group to enter the room, but not the first to take breakfast. Exhausted and hungover after the events of the previous night, he gazed around the room. It was a dazzle. His eyes stung and struggled to focus. Bob picked out a single figure sitting alone at the table closest to the window. It was the tall man that he had seen in the reception lobby when they had first arrived and at other times in the restaurant. Bob waved in acknowledgement.

The well-dressed man waved back. Bob's eyes now in focus, he observed that the man sat with a very upright posture, a straight back. The man's gray hair parted and styled in a classic 1940s look. He wore a white button-down shirt under a tailored but worn jacket. Bob noticed the purple lining and thought that the jacket must have been an expensive item when purchased, it still had a certain style, maybe it was Italian.

"Good morning." Said Bob, calling out to the man as he approached his table.

"Good morning to you. I am Peters, by the way." Responded the man, his voice had a hint of an accent that Bob could not quite place. But it was of European origin, he was certain.

"Hi, I am Bob, I am here with the student group."

They shook hands. Peters had a very firm grip, which surprised Bob. He did not expect such strength from an old man.

"You're here for this week too?" Asked Bob.

"No, I am here for a long time, many years now. I come to this place in 1965."

"You here for all that time? That is thirty years! Can that be true?"

"Yes, it is true."

Peters pushed the remnants of his breakfast around on his plate with his fork. The egg hard as a rock moved like a rook on a chess board, the sausage the color and texture of a dry cigar.

"Did you enjoy your visit out yesterday?" Said Peters.

"Oh, you mean our bus trip out into Sneaton Thorpe, that village near Whitby. Do you know it?"

"Yes, I know it very well, very well. I know the church, and I did some work at a warehouse there for some friends I know. Some time ago. It was in a farm business. I worked in the production office there, we made some good things."

"I think that might be the place that we went to there. To the Whitby Rock place? That is an unusual place, and so is that village."

"Yes, well heck, yes, but now that explains something." Peters paused, his head turned, and he stared out of the hotel window. His fork dropped from his hand and clattered onto his plate as he continued to speak.

"It is a long, long story. But you need to know it now, for a reason. Heck, I am thinking, that will be clear to you. You saw it last night."

Peters looked back at Bob with a gaze of expectation. Bob knew Peters needed to let him know something important. Maybe it would be useful for his report.

"OK, I am interested to hear. Let me get some breakfast and I will come straight back."

"Well, that is OK, because I have something about this thing, something when before I first came across to here. Save this table, I will be a moment back. You will like this, I know it."

In the meantime, Jack, and Chris both entered the Deck and Bob joined them in the line for breakfast. Russ followed close behind but did not make it further than two steps into the room. The moment that he saw Peet, turning in one movement, Russ pivoted a half circle on his heels and left. He followed Peters into the reception lobby. Bob turned to Jack.

"He is an unusual character, that one."

"Try sharing a room with him, constant babble. I go to sleep, and he is talking. When I wake up, he is talking, I am sure that sometimes it is the end of the same conversation that we started before I dozed off. This morning he was mumbling as I woke up, 'Stop nibbling my arm!' he was saying."

"You were nibbling his arm?"

"No, that was his random stuff, sleep talking. I hope." Said Jack.

"Anyway, I wasn't speaking about Russ. I am talking about the old guy, you know, the tall guy who hangs around here. He has gone to get something out of his room, I think." said Bob.

"Oh, what about Tony, is he OK, did you settle him down?" Said Jack.

"Yes, he is sleeping it off. Best not mention anything about it when you see him. He spent half of the rest of the night standing in the bathroom and looking at himself in the mirror. He still had the pile of dirt on his head."

"Sounds like the start of a psycho movie."

"Bob, what have you been up to now? You are always chatting away with random folks, what's going on with the old guy?" Said Chris.

"Come on, you know me, I just like to hear about people's stories. I think he is just a lonely old guy; he has been here since 1965. 1965! At this hotel!"

"What in the same room?"

"Who knows, he is coming back now, let us see. He just needs someone to talk to."

Peters returned, he gestured at Bob to return to the table.

Bob, Chris, and Jack complete their breakfast selection. Peet stared at each of them as they passed and made no secret of doing so. The three headed over to the table where Peters had steadied himself at his chair. He sat back, the chair creaked, his head bowed, and his hands held together as he lent forward to say a prayer. He whispered:

"Guide me through this abyss of compassion and pity and grant me the goodness and fortune which you displayed to the good thief."

45
OVERTURE

s it the sense of adventure that pushes men and women to undertake deeds which they would, in all other circumstances, brush to one side? Or is it from a need greater than which can only be satisfied with urgency?

Peters finished his whispered prayer and raised his head. He stared at the three as they approached the table, pulled the chairs, and sat with their breakfast selections.

"These are your friends? Your good friends?" He said to Bob.

"Yes, this is Chris and Jack."

"Guys, this is Peters he is also at the hotel."

"Yes, very good in meeting all of you. Please, all sit here. Heck, there is plenty of space."

"I hear you have been here a long time. That is a lot of breakfasts and dinners. How do you manage that? How is your digestion?" Asked Chris.

"Ha, yes, well heck, you get used to the food. It is terrible. Heck, but I have had much worse than this here. Much worse."

Peters arranged his knife and fork side by side and together on the plate and pushed it into the center of the table. He picked up his coffee and took a sip, slurping.

"I am not so sure about that." Said Chris, as he played with a burnt sausage and rolled it about his plate. It made a strange metallic noise as it turned on the porcelain, like steel on a lathe. He knew that any attempt to spear it with his fork or cut it with his knife had the potential to launch a fragment across the room, with the potential of injury to an innocent passer-by.

"Let me get to the story I have. It is long with many things put together by chance, but you will see it all. It is all true. I think you will know how we all can use it." Said Peters.

"A long time ago. I was in my thirties and I had finished my lecture work at the university in Gothenburg. That is Sweden, you know that of course. I had needed some ways to make money in quick time. But it was a risk, and I depended on others."

"That is what I need to do now." Said Chris.

"So, heck, one thing led to another. I ended up here. You know, many people came over to the docks for work, in Hull. The last place I was at in Sweden was a small town called Lysekil. It is on the coast, a little town. Not much happens there, much like here though. Well apart from…"

Peters hesitated and looked out of the hotel window, and his long fingers reached into the inside pocket of his jacket. Before he could speak again, Bob interrupted.

"Apart from what?"

Just as Bob finished his words, Peters pulled out a folded piece of paper folded into precise quadrants, dropped it onto the table and unfolded it. He pressed it flat with the palms of both hands. Folded so many times, the creases in the paper stood up like the white caps of waves in the ocean. Over time, the typeset printing had become smudged and faded. Flattened the best it could, he picked up the newspaper remnant and thrust it into Bob's face. Bob moved backwards in his chair, almost pushing it onto two legs. He regained his balance.

"OK, what is this?" Said Bob.

"It is an old newspaper article. I have had it a long time. It is what has happened before that when I came here."

"It is in Swedish though, isn't it?"

"Yah, it is Swedish. I shall read it for you. I will translate it."

Peters pulled his reading glasses down from their resting place on top of his head. He cleared his throat in preparation and read aloud.

"LYSEKIL NEWS. SATURDAY, AUGUST 28th, 1965. The Headline says so 'THREE YOUNG MEN DISAPPEARED'."

"Three men were all reported missing at various times by different people during the last week in July. The authorities did not realize until later that the three men may have been together when they disappeared." Said Peters.

He paused again, peered over the rim of his glasses. He assessed his audience was ready for the next instalment.

46
HEADLINE

T he establishment educates journalists in the art of storytelling to lead with satisfying headlines and allow the facts to take care of themselves, if at all. The inverted pyramid of importance within their newspaper writing reveals value in descending order. Read an article and pay consideration to the last because it is natural that it should be the first.

Inside the Deck, the four; Peters, Jack, Bob, and Chris remained at the breakfast table, Peters read the newspaper article out loud. Jack, Bob, and Chris paid attention while they attempted to consume the food in front of them. The article set out the mystery disappearance of three young men and where their car was last seen. The text laid out the mystery but did not paint the picture in full, Peters helped them to compose the event.

Thursday, July 29, 1965 was a drizzly afternoon just after 8 p.m. on Kungsgaten in Lysekil, Sweden. The rain was light, but it was enough to form medium-sized beads of water on the waxed blue paintwork of a parked a two-door Volvo PV44. 'Downtown' by Petula Clark played on the car radio as the vehicle sat with its engine running. The wipers squeaked as they moved back and forth to clear rain from the screen, providing intermittent occasions of visibility. A swirling plume lifted itself from the exhaust and the cloud clung to the rear of the vehicle like the cloak on a hangman's back. The song was a hit that year, played loud enough on the street to hear. But no-one did as the street was empty.

Gus, the driver of the car, stared at the apartment block and the street level cafe opposite. The tables outside deserted because of the rain. A few customers had taken cover from the weather and huddled inside the cafe. He could just make out their form through the condensation that obscured the glass in its facade. His focus soon returned to the large doorway adjacent, the primary access to the residential units above. Erik was late, they had been waiting for some time. Gus sounded the horn twice in a quick succession. Curious eyes within the cafe turned in inquisition of the car and its occupants. Gus did not need the attention and looked away, shielding his face.

"Where is he? We told him eight-thirty." said Gus.

"He will show up, you know he is never on time." replied Josef, who was in the passenger seat.

The door to the apartment block opened and Erik stepped out, his jacket held above his head with both arms extended, like he was surrendering to an enemy force. He ran to the car without avoiding the puddles.

"Look, here he is! He cares more about his hair than being on time or getting his feet wet." Said Josef.

∞⚜ 211 ⚜∞

Gus rolled the side widow down. A mix of drizzle and spray from the wipers met him full in the face as they cleared the water from the screen. He closed his eyes and shouted.

"Come on, Erik, get in. We need to get there by eleven tonight!"

As Erik got to the car, Josef jumped out and moved the passenger seat forward to allow Erik to squeeze into the rear seat. As soon as Josef closed the door, the car took off before Erik had settled himself and the momentum of the vehicle threw him backwards into the seat. He sank into the springs, then hauled himself forward to sit upright.

"Sorry, our sister was just here. She was checking in. Left me some food and clothes."

"That sister of yours takes care of you, man." Said Gus. "She can look after me anytime."

Erik clipped Gus on the side of his head with the outside of his right hand.

"Careful what you say there, boy."

"Calm down guys, today is a big deal. A big deal. It's going to take us over one and a half hours to get down there, so settle down and enjoy the ride." Said Josef.

Gus Nielsen, 22, Erik Holm, 21 and Josef Holm, 19, all worked at the Gothenburg docks together. Their job was to load and unload various shipments as they arrived or departed the dockside. The compatriots had found favor with a local consortium who controlled the trade there. Contraband items passed through without issue if they oiled the proper channels. The three had agreed and engaged themselves to facilitate the loading of certain items onto boats without the correct papers for a significant reward. No questions asked, nor should they be, or they would be in immediate danger. Now they were on the way to the docks in Gothenburg to pick up a special cargo.

The car continued south along the road route towards Gothenburg and passed through the town of Uddevalla, the surrounding landscape and valley masked by the low clouds and diminishing visibility. Uneventful, the journey completed, the vehicle arrived at the docks and the Ringon industrial area in Gothenburg just before eleven. They had made good time. The businesses had finished most of the activity in the area for the day some hours prior to their arrival. It was dark, and without industry, eerie silent.

"Who are we meeting?" asked Josef.

"We have a pickup for the boss, I have not been here before." Said Gus.

"Here we go guys, let me do the talking. Come with me."

All three got out of the car together, the motor running, and wipers and lights on. The rain dashed its form against the halo of a streetlight and the indigo sky beyond. They walked towards the warehouse, the headlights from the car projected elongated shadows onto the front of the building as they approached the door. Gus stopped before the rusted metal roller shutter frontage of the building and knocked on the panel hard with his fist. The sound amplified by the corrugated steel rattled back louder than the effort that he had applied.

"Wait there!" A voice from the other side of the door and inside the warehouse shouted in return.

A small rectangular opening in the door slid sideways to reveal a pair of somber brown eyes set in bloodshot rims. The lifeless orbs set straight at Gus without blinking, shifted to peer either side of him.

"What is your business here?"

"My name is Gus. I am picking up a package for the boss. You should expect me."

"And who are they?"

"It is OK, they work with me, we are all together."

"Who is the boss?"

"Bridget."

"Wait then." Said the voice. The opening closed with a clunk.

"You got to be kidding me. I'm getting soaked here." Said Josef.

"Just hang on." Said Gus.

The steel door opened, accompanied by a shrill mechanical noise and rusty scraping of chains. The man, stocky, unshaven and in his mid-thirties, appeared with an aluminum briefcase. He handed it to Gus.

"You know what you need to do, yes? And where this goes? This needs to be on the boat tomorrow."

"Yes, no problem. We will get it on the boat."

"The boss expects it. So, it had better happen." said the man from the warehouse, turning without speaking, into the warehouse. The door closed behind him, accompanied again by the shrill shriek of metal against metal.

Gus returned to the car. The others followed.

"A real charmer, that guy." Said Josef.

"You do not want to mess with him. Let us get out of here. Open the trunk, Josef." said Gus.

"Let us go, I'm soaking."

Doors slammed closed; the car set off towards the docks. The men were not seen at their homes again by any of their families or friends.

47
FROGMAN

Peters paused his reading. For a moment, a silence hung over the breakfast table like a low mist on the moors. Jack, Bob, and Chris considered the tale of the circumstance that led to the disappearance and their own visualizations of it.

"Were you one of the missing men?" Asked Bob.

"No, no, heck no, I was not one of those guys. Let me read more and onto the following news."

Peters hesitated, as to get his breath, adjusted his glasses and continued to read the article. He knew they were now hooked.

"The headline is 'DISAPPEARANCES LINKED TO THE FROGMAN BANK ROBBERY?'"

"You were the frogman?"

"No, no, heck no, I was not a frogman!"

Peters responded, frustrated. He paused and glanced out of the hotel window to recover his composure before he continued with a full voice, soon lowered to be only just above a whisper.

"Two robbers, one of them a man dressed as a woman, the other a woman dressed as a man."

"You dressed as a woman?" Asked Bob.

"No, no, heck no, I was not dressed as a woman. Please now, just quiet, as I was saying." Said Peters, for the moment, his voice raised.

"Two robbers, one of them a man dressed as a woman, the other a woman dressed as a man. Stormed a bank on the canal close to the Trädgårdsföreningen, Gothenburg after 2pm on July 29th."

To all, in appearance a man and a woman walked hand in hand, albeit with unusual and awkward gait, along Trädgårdsgatan a narrow, stone cobbled street. Although contained at its sides by tall buildings, the orientation of the street allowed the sun access at this time of day. It was full in their faces as they squinted towards the still water of the canal in front. The cobbles led to Bastionsplatsen and then to Stora Nygatan and their target, a branch of the Handelsbank on the right. The woman carried a black hold-all.

As the pair stood at the door of the bank, they each removed from the hold-all, a compact model-12 Berretta sub-machine gun, checked, and cocked for action. They entered the main entrance door into the lobby of the bank with guns raised. No one yet had regard of their arrival.

A well-illuminated space, the lobby opened into a color subdued decorated room, designed to confer financial confidence in the institution. High ceilings held ornate plaster coving and a single hanging crystal chandelier. The bank set tables and chairs close to the window area to receive the best light, at which one man sat and considered paperwork. A customer stood at the transaction counter, behind which sat three bank clerks. In a separate room to the rear of the main bank area, and also further behind the counter, was the managers' office.

The manager, Mr. Lofgren, sat at his substantial oak desk, on it a leather writing pad, a lamp, and photos of his family. He had been in the same office for almost thirty years, with nothing of any consequence happening in the bank for all of that time. It was only three months away from his retirement. He would be moving to his cottage in Nordkroken, overlooking Lake Vänern, north east of Gothenburg. Complete with its wide sandy beaches, and shallow coves.

Stina was in her twenties and stood at a height well above her companion, even without heels. Gun in hand and dressed in a man's dark gray business suit, with her hair tied under a fedora hat, she looked like an American mobster. Varg was smaller in statue, he wore a skirt and blouse which covered an ample and full chest, a dark brown wig completed his disguise. They had arrived to take care of the chief business of the day.

48
ROBBERY

After two steps, both robbers let off a volley from their guns towards the lobby ceiling. The bullets ripped through the plaster, mincing it into small segments, now released to the hand of gravity. Dust and chunks of ceiling fell and landed all around and covered Stina and Varg.

"Everybody stand where you are." Stina shouted, coughing through the dust.

"That has gone right down my bra." said Varg. He pulled a substantial chunk of ceiling out of the front of his low-cut blouse and threw the debris over his shoulder.

"Yes, everybody on the floor."

"Stand on the floor. Do as I say, and we will all be OK."

"Just tell them to stay still and not to move."

"I said that. I said that."

"No, you did not, you said to stand on the floor, they are all standing on the floor, they're not floating."

"Never mind that, let us just get on with it, fast."

Varg hitched up his skirt. Moved towards the counter, vaulted, and cleared it in one leap. He landed at the side of the first bank clerk, a young man in his 20s.

"You are not a woman." Said the clerk in surprise.

"Neither are you, is that a problem?"

"No, Miss."

Standing beside the bank clerk, Varg opened his blouse and produced a bag from his right bra cup and handed it to the clerk.

"All the money in here, now. All of it!"

Varg slid over to the next clerk, a woman in her thirties. He rummaged in his blouse and from the remaining full bra cup produced a similar bag to the first. He handed the bag to the clerk and patted flat the now deflated bra cups.

"I know, it is just not your size, darling. Fill the bag, everything you got! Including the hidden drawers, and no, not yours, the hidden ones, I know you have them down there."

By this time, the bank manager had heard the commotion and peered with some hesitation through the small, glazed window in his door. and then moved to pull a small bottle of Brännvin from his desk drawer. A potent beverage distilled from fermented potatoes and seasoned with anise and cumin. As its flavor described, the liquid could remove the varnish from the most polished of furniture. He crawled under his large and ornamental oak desk, taking one photograph of his family with him. The bottle held, he removed the cap and in one movement took the largest gulp that he could accommodate. The fingers of his left hand searched the underside of his desk like a spider hunting a fly. He found and pressed the alarm button. The bell sounded, it was loud, and it distracted the robbers for a second.

"The alarm! Come on, get on with it." Said Stina. She patrolled the lobby with her gun raised and wandered close to the man who crouched at the table. Stina looked over to Varg as the alarm sounded. The man 'Thunder Thor' a professional wrestler, pounced. Thunder, to his fans, was in his forties, stocky and very agile. He grappled Stina around the waist with both hands, and they both were on the floor in a matter of a split second. They threw chairs and tables as they thrashed and rolled around on the floor. Stina held the gun in her right hand, she ended on her back and in a moment, with a quick trademark wrestling move Thunder got the better of the contest. He straddled Stina, sitting on top of her with all his weight and his knees at either side of her.

"You are not a man!" He said.

"Is that a problem?"

"It is for you!"

"No, you mean for you!"

With no other option available to free herself, Stina squeezed the trigger of the gun still held in her hand and fired off a single shot. As the round left the chamber and travelled down the barrel, its direction set. The wrestler winced and grimaced, even though the pain had not yet reached his sense.

"You shot me!" The wrestler screamed. He now felt the pain, the burning hot metal sent through his knee, shattering its cap. He rolled off her and gripped the joint of his leg, his clothing already soaked with the warmth of his own blood.

"I shot myself, Oh no! I shot myself, no, no, no." Screamed Stina. The bullet had passed through the wrestler and had lodged in her right leg, just above the knee.

The wrestler continued to writhe and groan on the floor. Stina grabbed an overturned chair and with some strength and more determination. She pulled herself to her feet, it hurt. Varg collected the now full bags and with urgency climbed back over the counter with them in hand.

"I told everybody on the floor." Said Stina. She waved her gun around the bank.

"Do not be as stupid as that idiot!" Said Varg, brandishing the gun with no aim.

"Come on. We got to go. Now!" Said Stina.

"OK, OK, can you walk?"

"Oh, I can go, yes, go." Stina limped as they walked out of the bank and into the bright sunshine that burned their eyes and illuminated Stora Nygatan. They turned left towards a set of steps that led down into the canal. Varg held two bags and hitched up his skirt. Several of the bank employees emerged as a group onto the street. They stopped for a moment and without saying a word to each other jogged toward the robbers.

On reaching the steps, Stina and Varg striped away their clothing. The dress came off, followed by the large elasticated bra which Varg threw over his shoulder like a catapult. Hidden beneath their disguises and revealed wet suits and snorkels as they removed their clothing. Two of the bank staff ran to the canal wall, they threw whatever they could lay their hands on at the robbers, most of it coming out of a nearby dumpster. A hail of empty cans, bottles and half eaten burgers flew around the robbers as they entered the water. The sound of police sirens got louder and closer.

"Shoot over their heads!" Said Stina, she gasped, out of breath and in a pain that she had never felt before. Nausea hit her, she could feel the warmth of the blood as it tricked down her leg and engorged her wetsuit.

"We need to get into the water now, we'll miss the pickup boat."

Varg turned toward the bridge while he waded, stepping backwards into the water. He fired a burst from his sub-machine gun over the heads of the pursuing clerks. The volley of gunfire forced the clerks to retreat. The sound of police sirens in the distance now heard above the noise of the traffic on the roadways nearby.

"We got to go right now." said Varg.

"You go, swim, now, swim. I will find you later. At the meeting point we agreed in Lysekil, you know it."

Varg, with both bags in hand, waded into deeper water and disappeared. Stina, now finding it difficult to stand, lurched into the water and headed for the reed filled shallows on the opposite tree lined bank, next to the Trädgårdsföreningen, a park, glass house and paths. She submerged, hoping no-one would find her. The tip of a snorkel and blood-stained water revealed her location, and they discovered her without too much effort.

"Even with this, The Robbers left the bank with the bags containing over twenty thousand Kronor. That was about 100,000 now in today's cash." Said Peters.

49
PLANNER

W hat is a planner anyway? Maybe it is someone who can look at the past and see the future, a strategic clairvoyant. Someone who uses strategic thinking to ensure that the overall process moves towards a rewarding outcome. Someone who sees opportunity but quantifies the risk.

In the Deck Peters pressed his spine straight against the back of his chair, his joints gave a couple of snaps as he stared out of the window. Not finished with the tale, he needed the taste of adventure to be the foundation of the next instalment, a psychological dessert. Peters attention returned to the table. Bob had a puzzled look about him, an appetite to hear more. He was working on a question; Chris had given up manufacturing his breakfast out of whatever was on his plate, and Jack poured over the newspaper article to gauge its authenticity, even though he could not read a word of it. The texture of the paper felt right between his finger and thumb.

"You, you, were the wrestler?" Said Bob.

"No, no, heck no, I wasn't the damn wrestler!" Replied Peters.

"I guessed it then, you, you, were one of the bank clerks?"

"No, no, heck no, I wasn't the damn bank Clerk!".

"Oh so, you, you, were the robber? Were you?"

"Well heck no, no, no, I was not the robber there!" Peters looked to the ceiling, placed both hands on his head and exhaled a loud gasp.

"Give me some of this strength. I was not in the bank."

He hesitated. Pressed back in his chair again.

"When they had got away, they should have swum to a boat to the escape."

"You were in the boat then?"

"No, no, heck no, I was not in the boat. Please, no more question! No more question! Look now, I was waiting in my car on the main road near Slussbron, the bridge over the same canal. From there we could drive towards the Ringön industrial district then connect north to the roadway system to Lysekil."

"As I thought, you were in the gang; I thought that I did, right from the start."

"Finally, finally, yes. I was in the gang. I was the planner in that raid."

"You were a planner? We are planners too." Said Bob.

"He doesn't mean town planner; he means bank robbery planner." Said Jack.

"I know, I know. Anyway Peters, did you get away with the money? Is that why you are here?"

"No, heck, no, they caught the rest of the team with all the cash. It was a waste. You have known now; the one had shot herself in the leg with her own gun when one of the bank people wrestled with her. They captured the fool in the river after. She could not swim away because of her leg and the bullet there. The other swam to the boat, picked up by another member of our team.

He had waited on the canal closer to the Palm House, it is a greenhouse in the Trädgårdsföreningen park. They got away but could not make it to me because by then the police were all over the city center. There were swarms of them. They were both caught on the canal trying to get out into the river. I saw this from the car. I left fast after that."

50
RIDE

The newspaper had spent the headline; the facts twisted and framed to form a complete story, but it was not yet all in place. How could it be told? Many details and events were still unreported. Because at the time they were unknown to anyone but to the three missing men and their companion. Peters continued the story.

"I realized the bank robbery had failed; The whole thing unfolded in front of my eyes from Trädgårdsföreningen park. I would need to head north as soon as possible. The police were setting up more patrols, and I was not sure if they had seen my car waiting or escaping the area. I could not risk being stopped; I had a reason for travelling but did not need the attention."

"The route between Gothenburg and Lysekil passed through many towns and villages, each presented an opportunity where they could stop me. As I neared Kungalv, a short distance outside of Gothenburg, I determined that would be a good place to abandon the car and try to hitch a ride north. I caught sight of a track as the headlights found it, it led to an old barn. I turned off the roadway. The area seemed to be uninhabited, so I maneuvered the car out of sight from passing vehicles."

"I remained in the car for a while, hoping that the weather would ease, and considered my next move. I switched the lights and the wipers off. The rain drops on the screen turned to miniature rainbows as they diffused the overspill light from passing headlights. Cars passed by on the road, in both directions and at steady intervals, then after a while there were none. The weather had not let up any, so I set out to walk. Wary of police patrols I held tight to ditches and hedgerows in case I needed to hide. I kept a lookout for approaching headlights, both ahead and behind. By that time, I was cold and wet, and I pulled the overcoat tight and lifted its collar around my neck to keep out the drizzle. It helped a little, but not enough. I knew I would need to find something soon."

"I glanced behind and saw car headlights approaching in the distance. There was a ditch and I turned towards it. But then I halted as I picked up a sound of a song, something by the Rolling Stones hanging between the gusts of wind. I calculated that this could not be a police car, they would not be playing the radio, not that loud anyway. The car passed me, then stopped and reversed to be just ahead of where I stood. I did not move. It was too late to evade the three occupants who that I saw silhouetted inside the vehicle against the lights of the distant town."

"The side window of the car closest to me wound open. The music increased in volume. A head appeared and shouted above the combined noise of the car engine, radio, and wind. I could just hear it say."

"Hey there, you need a ride?"

It was Josef. Also in the car was Gus and Erik. They were returning from the pickup they had made earlier in Gothenburg.

"That would be nice, if you have the room."

"Sure, you will need to get in the back, where are you headed?"

"I was on my way to Stromstad." Said Peters. That was his cover story. His home was in Gothenburg, but he needed to steer clear of that for a few days. Just in case the Stina or Varg should talk.

Josef opened the door and pushed the seat forward, Peters climbed into the rear seat beside Erik. Peters was wet and tired, but he knew he would need to befriend the occupiers with conversation during the ride. The door closed, and the car continued its journey.

"Thanks for stopping. I was getting soaked out here. Heck, my car broke down back there."

"We are on our way home to Lysekil. There is no way you will get to Stromstad tonight. That is miles away."

"Maybe I can find a Hotel in Lysekil and get a mechanic for my car tomorrow?"

"There is the Grand hotel, you could get a room there, and Birger is an excellent mechanic in the town." Said Gus.

"No need, hey, you can stay at my apartment tonight, I have plenty of room and dry clothes." Said Erik.

"And we are coming back to Gothenburg tomorrow, we could drop you there to get your car fixed." Said Gus.

"That's very kind of you. Heck yes, that would be very kind. Thank you."

"What were you in Gothenburg for?" Asked Josef.

"I am a lecturer at the Chalmers University. My course ended last week, and I am on my way home now."

"Chalmers, eh? What were you teaching?"

"It is Chemical Engineering. I lectured. But now I hope to get another job in the area to get some good money."

"Hey, you know what, you could. Well, we all work in the docks, it's a simple way to get some cash fast." Said Gus.

"Not the only way." Peters Said, to himself.

"We can get you in there, man, we can take care of it. It is good money. We know people. Good people." Said Josef.

In the Deck, Peters continued to read from the article.

"It was not long after they all disappeared, Erik's sister reported she had gone to his apartment. She had met a man there that she had not seen before."

51
APARTMENT

I n the Deck, the story was continuing to unfold in the imaginations of the three listeners, as if the article itself had taken the form of a folded origami swan, whose wings flapped as Peters pulled the tail. Peters had described the history; the students were each creating their own mental construction of the happenings.

"We got to the apartment in Lysekil; it was late. They invited me to go to the bar with them, but the day had exhausted me. They all left and went there themselves. Erik left me some dry clothes, and I went to sleep on the couch. The morning came, and they were not there. I do not think they came back that night, or they left very early. I stayed there a couple of days and waited. It was a useful opportunity to stay low, away from the cops. That is when the sister came to the door." Said Peters.

It was Monday, August 2nd, 1965, just after 8:30 a.m. Britt entered the doorway to the apartment block beside the café on Kungsgaten and started up the three flights of stairs to Erik's apartment. Britt was the older sister to Erik and Josef; she was twenty-six and often stopped by to check on Erik on her way to her work at the pastry store in the town square. It was the start of a new week and she had not spoken to Erik since she had seen him on the Thursday before. That was not like Erik, he would call her to chat about the week on his days off if they had not spoken in person.

She stood at the apartment door, caught her breath, and knocked. Britt had a key but always checked first before she entered. There was no reply. She rummaged in her shoulder bag for the key. Her fingers hit everything in her bag except what she required. She knew she should take all of this stuff out of her bag; it would make it so much easier. Britt, after some effort, found the key and moved forward with her arm outstretched to push it into the lock. Before she could, the door handle rattled, and the lock released from inside. The door opened. It was Peters. Britt took a step back, surprised, her arm with the key in hand pointed at a stranger's face. She did not know who the man was.

"Oh, hello. I am looking for Erik. I am his sister. Britt."

"Hi. Sorry, he is not here, he said he was going to the café in Hamngaten Square with Josef and Gus, they have not been back."

"So, you know all the guys? And Josef, too? I don't think I know you?"

"Yes, I know them, but not for long. They helped me."

"Isn't that Erik's sweater?"

"Oh, yes, he let me borrow it."

"Well, be careful with that, I made it for him, it's special. The café in Hamngaten Square, you say?"

"Yes, that's what he said. Do you want to come in and wait?"

"I am on my way to work. I can check there on my way."

"OK, I will tell him if he comes back before you find him."

"Alright, thank you. I will go down there and see if I can catch him. Yes. Please let him know I have been looking for him if he comes back before I get hold of him."

"Yes, I will do, bye now."

"Bye."

Peters continued to tell the story.

"Erik's sister then visited the café but no-one there had seen him, or the others. The police did not know that it was me, but now the sister could recognize me, she saw my face. Then I knew I had to leave town. As I was packing, Erik came back. He was in a state and very anxious."

"I need to get out of here! Fast." Said Erik. He ran around the apartment and gathered some items of clothing and some small valuables.

"Why?"

"I can tell you later, it you want to come. We are in trouble."

"Where are we going?"

"The docks, there is a freighter it will take us to England, Gus is waiting outside with the car. Come on."

52
DEPARTURE

This was unplanned. Peters had expected to stay low for a few days longer. But now Gus had returned to Erik's apartment in a panic, he knew that his life depended on what course of action he chose next.

"We need to leave, with me too. What is going on?" Asked Peters.

"The deal went bad. The boss thinks we betrayed him. He knows we picked you up and that you have something to do with this."

"But you know that is not right, don't you? I did not know you guys before now!"

"We know but the Society doesn't."

"The Society?"

"Yes, look, I don't have time to explain. Erik and Joseph are outside already in the car, Erik is in a bad way. He got beat up good. He told them we picked you up on the way here. They will be on their way."

The pair left the apartment with the few belongings that Gus had gathered and joined the others in the car waiting on Kungsgaten, in the same location as when it first left for Gothenburg five days earlier. They left in a hurry and headed to the caviar packing factory on Lysekil docks. There was no time to discuss what was going on, and Peters would depart with the others. He would find out more after they had got away from this place. Gus parked the car on the dockside where a freighter was being loaded in a hurry. The four left the car to board the ship. As they did, workers attached several heavy chains to the underside of the car and it was lifted onto the deck by a crane. Once aboard, the crew placed the four men in a cabin. Erik looked in a bad way, injured and bruised they were superficial but painful injuries.

"OK, so what is going on here?" Said Peters.

"We will tell you, but you know we are all in danger and we must get away from here until we have the chance to explain." Replied Gus.

"You need to tell me now."

"They stole the package that we had in the car last night. We did not know what was in the case. It was a lot of money. The boss blamed us and will not rest until we get it back or repay the sum."

"How much?"

"Fifty Thousand Krona. We have seven days."

"It would take more than a year to earn that much."

"Yeah, well, we are all dead if we don't get it back."

"Where are we going now?"

"This boat takes us to England. To Hull. We can hide there until we find out what we should do."

"I have an idea; I think I can help. It will make a lot of money if we can get them to help with this."

Peters shared his manufacturing concept with them and what he needed to set it up. They agreed it was the only way that they could even think of getting to a point to repay the sum and more. By the time the boat landed in Hull, the car had disappeared into depths of the North Sea. Of more importance, they had formed a plan to set up the mushroom growing and compound extraction factory. All they needed was the funding and a suitable location, somewhere that no one would notice.

53
MASTERMIND

There was a moment of silence as the many threads of Peters' story tied themselves together. A tangled knot that made some sense. It was almost time for the students to be called to the bus, now stationed in front of the hotel. All three were eager to hear more. Peters' knew that he had their interest, that was all that he needed. He had set the bait.

"Who else knows about this?" Said Bob.

"Only, only you three guys now."

"Why tell us?"

"Yes, why tell us now?" Said Chris.

"Because there may be a way for you guys to help me get back a package, it is in Sneaton Thorpe if you are interested, that is. I am too old to get it. It is too risky for me."

"Sneaton Thorpe? That is where we were yesterday!" Said Jack.

"I told him." Said Bob.

"And I think you visited the Whitby Rock shop, didn't you?"

"Yes, we did, remember, after the pub."

"We went into the shop. But no-one was there." said Jack.

"But you picked up some of that Whitby Rock, did not you?"

"Yes, how do you know that? I only have a couple of pieces, but I left some cash. I did not fancy any of the other stuff in there."

"Heck, you do have that Whitby Rock! Did anyone else get some? I need to see it."

"No, just me, I think. Yes, it's in my room."

"Why are you interested in the candy?"

"I know the reason that something that has happened. I think your friend might have also had some."

"What do you mean?"

"You know what he did? That tall guy. I heard; he was crazy. Heck, he was running around with a plant pot on his head, half naked!"

"You mean Tony? He had too much to drink more like."

"You will see. Before I tell you more, I need to know that all of this is between you and me. This is a secret."

"Won't say a word."

Chris and Jack nod in agreement.

"So, we all agree."

"Good, we will meet later. Can we get together at your room?

Peters pointed at Bob, without hesitation Bob replied.

"Yes, sure, it's room number eight, the 'OCTOPUS ROOM' on the second floor. Shall we say nine tonight?"

Bob, Jack, and Chris exchanged eye contact and nodded in response. Tresswell entered the Deck, today he had dispensed with his customary safari suit and replaced it with a hazmat style compendium complete with knee length rubber boots.

"OK, everyone. The bus is outside. Today is the visit to the organic pig farm. Make sure you have the appropriate clothing and footwear."

"Ken's bus will leave in ten minutes. This is the last day of field trips. Tomorrow you have a free study day to merge your research or do whatever you need to do."

54
JOB

An informative visit to a local pig farm had preceded Wednesday evening. The aroma of the day had attached itself to clothing, hair, and flesh. No one had escaped contamination. As a result, the students had spent the early part of the evening attempting to scrub themselves free of the taint; their effort had proved unsuccessful. A hanging stench of sweet air permeated the hotel from top to bottom, and all inside knew that this time it did not originate from the kitchen.

Jack and Chris had reconvened with Bob in his room to hear Peters' plan. Peters arrived. Every now and again he placed a folded handkerchief over his nose, hoping to dismiss the smell, or at least dilute its impact. The room was no different to any other in the hotel, but themed and decorated with images of the humble octopus, the eight-legged mollusk framed and set out around the room. All walls, no windows. The four arranged and sat themselves in a circle, using the beds, desk, and chair as a makeshift conference room.

"You understand I am telling you all these things because I want to work together to get what is mine there. This is my last chance. I have planned it all. There is a delivery tomorrow night. But that is not what I am interested in. I need to get all of my work. All the work that shows the process and the formula for the recipe."

Of the three students, Bob is contemplating the reasoning behind why he had gone this far. He was now sitting discussing plans for a robbery with a master criminal. He needed to know more, to convince himself.

"Is this illegal?"

"Well, I would not say that it is all good. But it is my things that we will be getting. They all belong to me."

"Yeah, but you know, none of us are criminals or have done anything like this before."

"And that is the best thing, no police records of you, any of you, yes? You are visiting and have another reason for being here. You are all invisible in this place. Nobody knows you; it is perfect. You are the ones I have been waiting for here all this time. I can get the equipment and I have a plan that will be simple to follow."

Peters felt the hairs on the back of his neck bristle as he imagined the plan. He had not felt this old friend, the rush of excitement, since he was much younger. A time when he himself took risks and made choices that would change his own life. His eyes dilated as the endorphins released into his brain. He enjoyed the moment and waited. Bob was not experiencing the same thrill and spoke up again.

"But none of us have done anything like what you want."

"We do not know what he wants yet. Let us hear what he needs us to do. And why? What is the full story? Tell us, Peters." Said Jack.

"Is there any cash in it for us? Why should we take the risk?" Asked Chris.

"Let me explain what the job is, and you can decide. But if you say no, then you say nothing to no-one. Not a bank robbery. Just a container of my work, my belongings. Let me start at the Whitby Rock shop and the door that leads from the back into the warehouse."

55
MUSHROOM

A muffled shout issued from the room adjacent put Peters on edge. He stopped to listen.

"It's only Aze, Pakistan must have taken a wicket. He's watching the cricket again." Said Chris.

"Behind and attached to the Whitby Rock shop is the warehouse. You can get there through the door from the shop. It is the grow house. It is very dark inside."

"Yes, it stank, I remember that." Said Jack.

"That is where the mushrooms are living. The boxes are full of good cow crap. They grow fast. It is perfect place."

"Mushrooms, so they market them, the mushrooms?" Asked Bob.

"No, no, not selling mushrooms. But part of them. Imagine the space now."

An aroma of fertilized dirt, rotting wood, and strong chemical filled the air inside the dark interior of the warehouse. Through a skylight above, a shard of light escaped through the blackout shutter and illuminated the agricultural nature of the processes involved within the room. Particles of soil and spores, disturbed by the slightest breeze, floated, caught, and reflected in the single ray of sun like aircraft marked by searchlight. Long waist high wooden beds, filled with thick, black, damp soil and wood chips, stretched the length of the space. Over each bed hung a metal tray, the underside of which contained lighting or heating elements.

A closer inspection of the contents of the beds reveals small clusters of off-white mushroom caps. In one corner of the room, a stack of boxes lay on a pallet next to a forklift vehicle. The boxes labelled 'Psilocybe Azurescens Spawn'.

"They do not sell mushrooms. But if you grow the correct type, they will be more value. They will make good LSD. What they have there is called Psilocybe. You may know them as the Magic Mushrooms." Said Peters.

"Yes. I have heard of those. People eat them to become high!" Said Bob.

"Yes, heck, yes. But it is more profit if you can separate the compounds from the mushrooms, they are like gold."

"They are making drugs?"

"How do you know all this?" Said Jack.

"Remember, as I spoke before. I am trained chemical engineer."

Peters paused between every sentence.

"Yes, they are making good LSD."

"Because it is a very special recipe. It is my recipe. I worked there in the laboratory for a long time. I know it all there. I set it all up. The Psilocybe Azurescens is a species of psychedelic mushroom his main active compounds are psilocybin and psilocin. If grown under the right conditions, he is the most potent of the tryptamine-bearing mushrooms. They contain compounds. I know they are the best, up to 1.8% psilocybin, 0.5% psilocin, and 0.4% baeocystin all in there, powerful."

"The laboratory, when you were at the university in Sweden?" Said Jack.

"No, they would have kicked me out of there if I had tried that. It is part of the story of how I got here. There is a laboratory connected to the Whitby Rock warehouse. I helped to build it."

"After the warehouse there is the laboratory, that's where I worked the most. I developed a way of isolating the LSD compounds by precipitating the amines from solution by using acetone. Nobody had that way of doing it, I was the first, in 1966."

"That sounds technical, but I can remember getting a whiff of the acetone. It smelt like a Korean nail salon." Said Jack.

"You should know that!" Said Chris. Peters continued.

"Once we had done that, we needed a way of getting it into the customer. That is where the manufacturing needed to be clever. The production room is through a door on the laboratory. I designed all of this room. Let me describe it." Peters painted a descriptive vision of the space.

A doorway in the warehouse's rear connected to the laboratory. The door opened to a bright room, and the light would spill out to illuminate the darkness of the warehouse. The laboratory looked like you would imagine it to be. Tables and workbenches filled with distillation apparatus and glass jars. Some connected to others, some containing liquid, others empty. They set the equipment up to synthesize the LSD compounds from the mushrooms. Vats of frothing yeast solution connect to larger transparent containers of the emulsified mushroom solution. The mixture is boiling, bubbling. Eventually, through a network of pipes and spiral connections, the evaporated solution loads a precipitation jar with gas. The gas condensed to a liquid is then dispensed onto trays where it dries to a solid. The solid is then ground by machine to a fine powder, ready to be incorporated into the recipe.

Racks lined of identical glass containers, each filled with a measure of the final synthesized compound, sit like a grocery store display of unbleached white flour. All ordered by the date of production and weight of the contents. The information printed on a small label on their face. From the laboratory a door opens into the production room, set up to create traditional seaside rock, the candy. The operation stores various ingredients in large dispensers and bags: sugar, glucose syrup, food coloring, flavorings, and jars of synthesized compound delivered from the laboratory.

A large metallic mixing vat of boiling water sits in the middle of the room. It is close to a water-cooled steel flat pan surface. A set of cutting shears sits on the table nearby. Off to the right is a "pulling" machine, at rest it appears to be a robot ready to waltz. One fixed arm, and two moving arms, one able to rotate clockwise, the other counterclockwise. Formed red colored lettering, "C I R H B O T W K Y", each the size of a small coin, lay on a steel worktop next to the flat pan.

"Once we had the compounds, we concentrated them into powder. But we did not have a safe way of getting the LSD out of the area. I had the idea that we make it to go into candy. If we did that, we could export it as good as food. So, the idea came to us to make the candy and use the lettering in that to carry the compounds."

"WHITBY ROCK!" Exclaimed Bob.

"Yes, that is it, that is it all. We make the lettering by adding the extracted LSD to the sugar. They make the rock candy like usual and it appears like normal candy."

"Why do you tell us all of this? So, what is it you need?"

"There is something that will make all of us better."

"Let me tell you more first. On Thursday evening a boat will arrive in Whitby quay from Sweden. It will carry two men. They will drive one man to Sneaton Thorpe to deliver a package. There he will exchange it for a delivery of a consignment of Whitby Rock."

"That is what we saw when we were waiting for Ken's coach at Whitby Quay, wasn't it? The guys in the boat, yes!" Said Jack.

"The exchange will happen in the pub. While that is happening, the production room and the laboratory are closed. That is when we can get to my documents. Here is what you need to do, I have it all planned. I will set up a van to use. Listen now to this."

Peter's detailed his plan; it would involve the use of a Whitby Rock van and for one of the three students to volunteer to get into the production room to grab the documents. Jack nominated himself, he would deliver the exchange and while the gang were busy head over to the warehouse to get the papers. He would head to the church, hide there, and be picked up by Peters later that night.

56
ALTERNATIVE

All plans are subject to timing and human variance. Jack returned to his empty room. He needed some help. Peters' plan did not create an alternative. He always planned an alternative, just in case. He picked up his phone and called the only person he knew could help.

"Hey, Crumb? It is Jack."

"Alright there. Bit busy at the moment, Jack."

Jack could hear Crumb breathing into the handset, heavy but shallow. A dog bark echoed in the distance. He could make out the metallic jangle of chains and he recalled that Crumb was on a gig. It was Wednesday, the night that they had asked him to drive for them.

"OK. Got it. I just need a minute."

"Yeah. Well, we are on a gig at the moment. Better make it snappy."

"Do you still have those fireworks?"

"Yeah, nobody wants to take any of them. The coppers have been sniffing around and the firework gig was on the local news. Did you see it? Made us look like right professionals, they did!"

"Something to put on your resume mate."

"What do you mean?"

"I mean, do you still have the fireworks?"

"Every single last one. They are all tucked away in Spud's mum's attic. Get off you stupid narl."

"What?"

"Not you, the dog. Get off me foot, me shoe, he has got my shoe! Spud, get me shoe off that mutt!"

"The fireworks, I can use them, can you get them to me?"

"Where?"

"Whitby. Tomorrow?"

"Whitby? Yeah, once I sort this dog out and get my shoe back. But we don't have transport, though. We can use our driver."

"No. I do not know them. You can use my car."

"OK, we can do that."

"You need the combination to the lockup. It is one, one, zero, seven."

"Like a secret agent?"

"No, not like that, one, one, zero, seven. The keys are inside under the passenger seat."

"Look, I have got me hands full at the minute. Text me."

"I will text now."

"Where are you anyway?"

"We are hitting the sausage factory."

"The sausage factory? Oh yes, you said."

"Yeah, we are onto some tasty pork links and pies!"

"And a butcher's dog, by the sound of it!"

"Oh, me nuts, you stupid dog. Spud! Get over here! Mmm."

The conversation ended. The phone silent, the connection dead. Jack messaged the details that will get the fireworks to where he needed them to be for the following night.

57
DECISION

Thursday was the day that the students could use for research and consolidation of their notes. The day passed without event. Just after 8:10 p.m. Jack, Bob, and Chris waited together halfway down a narrow alley that led to the rear of the hotel. A solitary streetlight threw out a worn yellow glow and captured the three huddled beneath it like moths to the moon. They shuffled their feet and kicked at the gravel, glancing at regular intervals to the alley's entrance from West Street.

"This is surreal." Said Bob.

"Yeah, we are all in the hands of an old guy that you befriended over a burnt sausage, flat eggs and soft toast." Said Chris.

"Don't blame me, I was just being nice. He's just a lonely man, all on his own."

"Because he had indigestion and gut rot from breakfast."

"Guys, this could be him now." Jack interrupted them. He was used to this. The moment before the tipping point, the point of no return. He knew what Bob was going through. Asking his moral self for confirmation, seeking reasons to justify doing what he was about to. Knowing and staying in the moment was the key here. Jack steadied himself. The plan was in place, no variation, and it would go as they wanted. He had a back-up.

The figure approached, a silhouette of a tall man. A shadow that flickered through the night like the twisting flame of a dying candle as he engaged the strips of focused light that illuminated parts of the alley. His long strides brought him closer; it was Peters.

"They park the van at the rear of the hotel. Down there." Peters pointed to the end of the alley and its darkest region.

"Here, these are the keys. Drive it to the quay. You know what to expect and what to do. They will be there at nine, you need to be ready."

"I am not sure about this. Not sure about this at all." Bob said. He was having second and third thoughts; he had done nothing like this before. Bob regretted becoming part of the scheme. The conversations they had over breakfast were now real. He was uncertain why he had committed to be a part of this. This was not a lonely old man; this was a master criminal.

"It is too late, it involves you. Even if you step away now. You will fail your good friends here. I thought you were the brave one." Said Peters. Gaslighting.

"Look Bob, if we stick to the plan then all you will need to do is drive the van, leave the rest to us." Said Jack.

"Ok, Ok. Let us go. I have to go right now." Bob snatched the keys from Peters' hand and headed down the alley towards the hotel. Peters turned and walked away in the opposite direction without saying another word as his shadow faded into the dark. The plan was in motion. Jack and Chris, flat footed, followed two steps behind Bob.

The three found the van where Peters had said it would be. It was white and had the livery and logos of the Whitby Rock brand set on its doors and sides. The evening was cold, but that was not the reason Bob's hands shook. Arm outstretched; fingers pinched the key and pointed towards the lock. The metallic tip of the key bounced off the paintwork two or three times before he found his aim and inserted the key to unlock the driver's door. Once inside, the van started without hesitation and all having boarded, headed towards Whitby quay and the interception.

The journey took about thirty minutes. The van arrived at the quay without incident and parked at the location that Peters had identified, close to the longest dock. With no sign of any activity, the three sat in the back of the van and peered out of the rear windows. It was dark, with a few boats tied up against the moorings. Everything was quiet apart from the lapping of the estuary tide as it washed against the dock pilings. Bob shook, he gripped his hands together to calm them. Chris rolled up his left cuff and glanced at his watch. The green luminous hands glowed. The time read 8:46 p.m.

"You sure it is at nine?" said Chris.

"That is what Peters said. Isn't it?" Asked Bob.

"Just stay calm, that is how we get this done. Do nothing that is any different from what we have planned." replied Jack.

"You, mean what Peters planned?"

"Wait, I think that this is the boat." Said Chris. In the water, a rowboat containing two men steered itself towards shore. The regular dipping of paddles broke the surface adding their own rhythm. The sound grew in volume as the boat approached.

"Look, there are two of them! Two of them in that boat! Peters said there would only be one! I do not know if I can do this. We can handle one, but two. No. two, that is too much. What if we get caught? I do not need to be doing this. No. Not this."

"Bob, we are here now; the plan is still the plan. Just wait, take a breath, and see how this works out. Come on, let us do this, no panicking now. We just need to take care of this guy and then get me to the warehouse." Said Jack.

"Ok, Ok, I am with you guys."

The rowboat arrived at the dock, bumping with a dull thud into the wooden deck. The two figures remain seated, their gaze set on the van.

"I'll get out and signal with the flashlight. Bob, you are right, if they both come over then we will just get out of here. So, get back in the driver's seat and get ready to go if we need to." Said Jack. He opened the rear door and signaled a series of flashes in the boat's direction.

The figure closest to the dock stood upright and with an unsteady stretch planted a foot on the dock, the boat drifted, and the gap between his feet widened. A moment of panic subsided as the figure stabilized the boat and his balance before being handed a small briefcase. The boat departed. Jack re-entered the van and closed the rear door.

"Ok, we are on. It is just one of them." Said Jack.

The man marched with purpose to the van, the rear doors opened, Jack and Chris leapt out to grab the man by both arms. They threw him onto the backboards before he cried out. The doors closed behind them as they climbed on board, scuffing the toes of their shoes in the struggle.

"Go. Go! Not too fast, though. Remember no names." Said Jack as he wrestled with the courier. The van drove away, the man in the rowboat unaware of what was in progress. It raised no alarm.

58
COURIER

A melee of arms and legs thrashed around, feet kicked and bounced off the inside of the van, the sides booming like a bass drum as they were hit. The turmoil in the back unnerved Bob. His hands shook, he gripped the wheel harder. He looked over his shoulder at the fight and the van swerved as he swayed on the steering wheel. Chris held on to the man's arms long enough to bring them together for Jack to quieten them with a zip tie. The flailing stopped as the man's ankles were subdued soon after. Thrown to one side without care, the attaché case landed with a weight that belied its size. Bob straightened the course of the vehicle and glanced in the rear-view mirror to see Jack place a black hood over the man's head.

"This is a big mistake. You all making big mistakes." Said the man.

"That is enough now. You will be quiet!" Said Jack.

"Be quiet and no harm to you."

Jack lifted the hood and placed a strip of tape across the man's mouth. He then took a pair of headphones and placed them over the hood and onto the man's ears, connected to a portable music player they allowed them to talk without concern.

"Be quiet and no harm to you."

Bob took a breath and stared at his hands as they gripped the steering wheel. The shaking had subsided, but had now replaced by the bulging contours of raised blood vessels. The road was empty, and the van continued towards Sneaton Thorpe. After the frenzy, there was now a stillness as the perpetrators caught up to reality and their breathing steadied. Chris patted down and searched the man; a phone and a wallet were the only items that he found. He emptied the contents of the wallet, English and Swedish bank notes, credit cards and a driving license spilled onto his lap.

"Let us see. What do we have here? Yes, a driver's license. Yes, look, he is Swedish, his name is Sven. It would be Sven, would it not." Said Chris as he climbed into the passenger seat and continued to empty the wallet. Jack took his blond wig from his pocket, an old friend, ready for adventure. He adjusted it into position on his head and became Udde, his Swedish cousin.

"You have his phone?" Said Bob.

"Yes, why?" Chris replied.

"Take the sim out."

"Why?"

"Well, that's what they do in movies. They cannot track it then. Just in case."

Chris rolled down the side window and threw the phone out.

"There you go. They cannot track us now."

Jack climbed forward and between them to use the rear-view mirror to adjust the wig.

"Will this do?"

"Perfect. Let's get to Sneaton." Said Chris.

After twenty minutes driving through hedge lined lanes, the village of Sneaton Thorpe lay ahead. The spire of St. Bridget's church piercing the horizon. Even in darkness, Bob could make out the form of the building. The van was home, its identity would not cause any concern. It belonged there, and no one would see anything out of place. Bob maneuvered the vehicle to the end of the street leading to the Wilson Arms, the meeting point, and parked. The light from the pub doorway and windows spilled out onto the roadway, otherwise in total darkness and silence, save the rustling of the branches in the wind.

"It is pitch black out here at night." Said Bob.

"That is good. You both know what to do. Take him out to the Moors and drop him off. Make sure that it is after 10.30 p.m. and he cannot get to anywhere without a walk. When you get back, drop the van on a street and walk back to the hotel. You should be able to get back by midnight, just act normal. I will see you in the morning at the hotel. Remember, keep calm. And do not talk too much in front of him."

"What about you? You are good with this?" Said Bob.

"Yes. Just stick to the plan. It will all be good if you stick to the plan. Do not call me."

"Good luck, hey do not forget the case."

"Almost!"

Jack grabbed the handle of the case and pulled. It was the first time that he had noticed its weight; the case was heavier than he expected, much heavier. The heaviness wrenched his arm, and he almost overbalanced as the case stuck to the floor of the van like a magnet. Putting more effort in releasing it, he carried the case to the rear of the van, opened the door, and made his way onto the street. His walk to the pub would take him past the church and graveyard of St. Bridget's. The Whitby Rock shop and warehouse were opposite and quiet.

Bob and Chris left to deposit Sven in the middle of the Moors. It would take them an hour to get to a point that would be remote enough. Urra, a desolate treeless landscape in the middle of the North Yorkshire Moors. On arrival, they would hand Sven dry and waterproof clothing to protect him from the environment. It would be hours to walk to the nearest village, which was the intent.

Jack stood in the shadow of the church and studied the street in all directions. There was no activity. He set out towards the Wilson Arms. A glance at his mobile phone illuminated his face for a moment as he also adjusted his disguise.

"Where are they?" Said Jack. His breath hit the cold air and formed a swirling veil as he whispered to himself. He gripped the handle of the case, the stitching embedded into his palm, and he entered the warmth of the pub.

59
DISGIUSE

Jack's project management experience had taught him that a planned activity never worked the way you expected it would. Preparation, the key to any project, he had prepared. They were following Peters' plan, but he had an alternative plan himself, just in case. The success of the scheme depended on others, and that was now his concern.

Steadying himself as he entered the warmth of the Wilson Arms pub, Jack took a deep breath. Behind him, the hanging sign squealed on its worn hinge as the door swung and closed to keep out the cold air. On this night, the bar was a different place than he and his compatriots had encountered earlier in the week. Now there were many more locals, drinking, chatting, and playing dominoes. Music from the jukebox competed with conversation and joke telling. The place had got some life. Jack aimed towards the bar; his eyes locked straight ahead.

"Hey, Jack! Over here!" A voice bellowed over the noise of music and chatter.

Jack turned, he realized too late that he should not have reacted, but he had. It was Spud, his height meant that his head stood over all others in the bar. Still stunned, Jack then saw Crumb; he and Spud were attending the slot machine in the room's corner.

"What have you done with your hair? You color it all new romantic like your sister-in-law!"

"Oh, no." Said Jack to himself, making hand gestures under his throat in an attempt to halt further conversation.

"Hey der, who is dis Jaq? You may be in der dark here. My name is dis Udde. No Jaq."

"Oh, sorry, man. His mistake!" said Crumb. He understood that the disguise was part of this plan. He needed to calm Spud.

"But it is you, Jack! We brought the stuff!"

"You dozy twonk, it's a foreign guy. See, you got a couple of cherries there."

Crumb pressed his right foot onto Spud's left toe, at the same time pointed towards the display on the slot machine to divert Spud's attention.

"Ow! Are you sure they are cherries; they look like grapes to me? Wow. I am colorblind aren't I."

"Keep it down, he does not wish to be seen with us. Didn't you message Jack when we got in?"

"No, I thought you had."

"Dozy twonk. Now concentrate. Keep playing."

Jack spun around and glanced at the locals; they were oblivious to the conversation. There was no sign they had discovered him. Jack continued to the bar and the familiar landlady standing behind. He noticed she had painted her fingernails in a different color, as she rapped them on the countertop in time to the music. She had not heard the exchange with Spud.

"What can I do for you?" She said.

"Hey dar. Can I get a rum and coke please?" Said Jack in his best Swedish accent. He dropped the case where he stood.

"Yes, you can, anything else?"

"Ja, I am Udde and am looking for dat Ricky. Is he near today, I have to meeting in person with him? He expects, yes?"

"Ricky. So, you are here to meet with Ricky?"

"Well, I coming to do some of business with him. tell him that Sven sent me here."

"I know Sven. I don't recognize you. Have you been here before?" She squinted, there was something about this guy, but she could not place what it was. Maybe these Swedish guys all looked the same.

"Hey no, but my friend, Sven, is more been here."

"So, what's up with Sven?"

"Oh Sven. He is not healthy now. So, I coming here instead to meeting with det Ricky. I have the case."

"You sure you've not been in here before?"

"No. Not before these day. Can I see where the men's rooms are placed here?"

"Yes, they are out the back there to the right. I will let Ricky know you are here."

The landlady pointed to a door at the rear of the pub. Before he made his way there, he signed to Crumb to follow. Spud played on at the slot machine. Jack entered the men's room and checked out that the stalls were empty and adjusted the wig in the mirror. Crumb arrived.

"Sorry, Jack."

"Yeah, great that was, should we add that to his colorblindness? Why didn't you message?"

"I thought Spud had."

"Did you bring the fireworks?"

"Yeah, they are in your car out the back. The lot."

"Look, this needs timing and you both need to be on this. Get the fireworks and spread them around the village, concentrate on the warehouse across the street. If I don't message you in ten minutes, start firing them at, what time is it now? At 10.15 yeah? I have to get into the back of the process area in the warehouse."

"10.15 Right you are. What are you going to do?"

"Never mind that. 10.15 and have the car ready to go at 10.20 in front of the graveyard. There's also a package in the graveyard we need to take."

"The graveyard? OK, 10.15 and they get the lot."

"Got to go, that landlady is suspicious already. Leave it a few before you come out yeah?"

"Yeah, good luck, Jack. We'll do our bit."

"You better had, there's no one to bail us out of this now. 10.15 yes?"

"10.15, yeah on the nail."

Jack exited the men's room. The landlady stood at the bar with Jack's drink. He looked at his watch, it displayed 21:57.

"Ricky is in the back. I think he is expecting you. You better go through."

"Very good, here I am on the way."

Jack makes his way with the briefcase to the back room. Ricky is in his fifties, overweight and balding. He sat behind an old kitchen table, he spoke with an accent and asked.

So, no Sven today?

"No, he is bad in der belly. He is doing the shits all over."

"Hmm. Nice. So, you got the cash? This is a substantial order that you are carrying."

"All inside here."

Jack lifted the case onto the kitchen table.

"Not here. Come with me then. We need to go to the lab. Bring the case."

"Why do we go there? Sven did not tell me dat."

"Don't you know what the deal is today? There is over two million in that case. We go to the lab. I do not want any mistakes here."

"OK, I will following you."

Jack waited for Ricky to show the way and followed him out of the rear of the pub. Jack looked at his watch, a red glow, 22:02. Peters' plan was falling apart.

60
EXCHANGE

The battered green door pushed clear of its frame outwards into the rear yard of the pub. Jack followed Ricky's step into the low mist encouraged to hug the ground by the cold dense air. Flickering from above the door, a lamp illuminated the yard but was of no real help but to provide a surreal edge to the moment. The path was narrow and took them on a circuitous route around waste bins and stacks of empty bottle crates to a gate which opened onto the street. Across the street, and in front as they emerged was the Whitby Rock shop. Jack glanced left and right, nothing; he hoped that Crumb and Spud had started their preparations, he would need them.

Now side by side and in lockstep, Ricky and Jack walked past the front of the building to an entrance door on its side and behind the shop. Ricky fumbled and then inserted a key into the lock and opened the door wide. It was the growing area, dark, warm, and damp with a powerful aroma of acetone. Jack stepped inside, Ricky followed, secured the door, and led the way through to a new doorway that opened into a bright room. It was the laboratory, as Peters had described. Stacks of equipment, boxes, and containers. The smell of acetone even stronger now. Jack required a moment to allow his eyes to adjust to the brightness. He thought to the reprographics room at work; the light was bright, but the laboratory was much quieter and there was no Angie. He raised his head to better expose his eyes to the brightness and to hasten their adjustment to the glare. As he did so, he noticed skylights above that appeared as black squares in the ceiling.

In the center of the room was a stainless-steel table, beside it a pallet stacked with containers ready to load. Ricky took up his position beside the table and directed Jack to the other side. They stood over it like poker players in a saloon, not knowing that one of them held the eights and aces of a dead man's hand.

"Here we are then. Now, the deal. Let me see the money." Said Ricky.

Jack lifted the heavy attaché case onto the tabletop. He looked at the case. For the first time he realized the locks only opened with a secret key, a series of four numbers. Jack froze. He did not know the setting; it could be anything. He steadied his thumbs over the twin release latches on the case and held his breath, not sure if they would open. He pressed them at the same time.

A loud click as the springs on the mechanism flung the latches open. Jack took a breath. He opened the lid to reveal that it was full, neat bundles of cash notes. English Pounds issued in 100-Pound denomination by the Royal Bank of Scotland. Jack had never seen a 100-pound note, but now here, adding to two million, was an entire case full.

Jack rotated the case on the stainless-steel surface to face Ricky, who pushed his right hand into its inside like a vet delivering a calf and pulled up a random wad of notes. Holding them close to his face, he flicked through them, close to his nose and sniffed.

"Smells good. Looks like it is all there. Close it up again. Now, you are going to need our van to get this to the quay."

"Guys, come in here now!" Shouted Ricky.

Two men emerged from an area behind the pallet and stood beside it. They had been there all along. Jack recognized them, the chef and server from the hotel. They must launder the money there, he thought. Would they see through his disguise? Jack avoided eye contact.

"The brothers here will give you a hand and get the money to the hotel. There will not be any trouble with these guys around. No messing."

Jack looked at his wrist. 22:12. He needed three minutes.

"Hanging on now. I should look at dat box before to check all is there."

"If you must. Boys take a box and let us open it, nice and wide, so he can see the lot. Then get the van ready."

"Wait, I will be choosing the box." Said Jack.

Jack walked to face the pallet and chose a box halfway down the stack. Peet and Pit extracted it with some difficulty and dropped it on the table beside the still open case. Peet left the room to get the van ready for its load. Ricky pulled a pocketknife from his jacket and slid it down the center of the box. The box opened to show its content, Whitby Rock candies, all wrapped in clear translucent cellophane. Jack glanced at his watch again, now 10:14. Peet returned to the laboratory.

"Boss, the van is not here." Said Peet.

"What do you mean?"

"It was at the hotel, but someone took it. We thought it was one of the guys who used it for the pickup, but it is not here."

Ricky, his right eyebrow raised, looked at Jack.

"How did you get here?"

"In the van, as I was told. It was Whitby Rock van. At the quay."

"Who was driving it?"

"I do not know the man. He took me to the pub there."

Ricky now sensed something was not right, but it made little sense. The money was there in front of him, but something did not add up. Jack knew that part of the plan was to get access into the production room and to Peters' work. He was uncertain if that could be achieved now. Ricky, frustrated, slammed his fists onto the tabletop. The case and the box both shook and continued to do so longer than they should.

The building rumbled and dust fell from the exposed timber rafters above.

61
RETRIBUTION

E xpanding within the view above the skylight, a spider's web of burning fingers immured the black sky, soon followed by a cacophony of discordant fiery explosions. The entire building rocked; with more explosions heard from all directions. In the laboratory containers and boxes flew off racks and shelving, one of which issued a glancing blow to Jack's head, dislodging the wig and placing it over one eye. A pirate if there ever was one.

"There is a wig. On his head. I know that guy, he is at the hotel!" Cried Pit.

"What the! Do not just stand there! Get the imposter!" Shouted Ricky. The explosions became more frequent and louder.

"Here we go! Right on time." Said Jack.

Jack closed the top of the case, and in the same movement spun it around and grabbed its handle with both hands. He swung it with both arms outstretched like an East German hammer thrower. It caught Ricky a glancing blow on the side of his face, sending him a step backwards and into the pallet, spilling boxes and their contents on the floor. Peet and Pit moved to make their way around the table. Jack regained his balance from the spin and kicked out at a container that was close-by. Its lid popped off, and it hit the floor. A powerful stench of acetone filled the air as the liquid contained within spilled out onto the floor. His pursuers slipped as the chemical dissolved the grip of the soles of their shoes. They both slipped, stumbled, grabbed, and flailed at each other as they fell. The explosions continued to vibrate the building, the flashes appearing overhead.

Jack ran, he knew he could not make it to the production room and the set of documents that Peters had directed him to. He needed to get out as soon as possible. Jack held the case under his arm and headed to the graveyard as fast as he could for the remaining package. He was close to the door into the Whitby Rock shop, which was behind him. Jack pushed it open and left past the counter, then into the street.

The night sky was full of fireworks and their colors, exploding at a low altitude, the explosions deafening and close. The silhouette of the church now brought closer by the continuing firework display. Jack entered the graveyard and headed toward the unnamed headstones, as directed by Peters, which he had also seen during the student visit earlier in the week. He arrived at the center stone, dispensed of the vase and flower arrangement, and clawed at the ground. His hands soon felt the cold of a stone slab and its edge. Jack pushed his fingers between the stone and the earth so he could raise it, to discover a box beneath, just as Peters had said. He extracted the container about the size of a shoe box, not aware of its contents.

In the distance, at the entrance to the Whitby Rock shop, Jack could see the figures of Ricky, Pit and Peet as they stumbled in the doorway. A firework flew towards the warehouse and hung in the air above it, but it did not explode, instead the firework plummeted towards the roof of the warehouse and a skylight above the laboratory. As it hit the window, the glass shattered.

The unexploded ordinance fell to the laboratory floor, landing in a large puddle of acetone that had spread its fingers to other containers of the same chemical. Like a cobra about to strike, the firework sat upright for a second until it ignited and exploded. Heavy vapor from the acetone hung in the air and acted as an accelerant to the fire, the bright yellow fireball expanded, ripped through the structure. The entire roof of the warehouse lifted off its rafters and for a moment settled on its crumbling supports. Jack looked over his shoulder, the rubble of the building obscured the figures of Ricky, Pit and Peet as it disintegrated around them as they tried to exit the building.

Peters' plan had been for Jack to head to the church and hide out in the belfry until he could collect him later that night. The events to now had rendered that option mute. The fireworks had put Jack's own escape plan into operation, he now depended on Crumb and Spud. He would meet Peters the following morning back at the hotel.

As the firework explosions subsided, the fires around the village burned on, more containers exploded into yellow flames as the fire raged through the warehouse, laboratory, and shop. Crumb and Spud arrived at the gates to the graveyard in Jack's car.

"Go, go, go." Said Jack as he threw the case and box into the car ahead of him before jumping into the rear seat.

"Hey Jack, we know what you always say, let us take it nice and steady to avoid attention." Said Crumb.

"Stuff that, let us get out of here, fast!" Said Jack.

"Just go, man. Put the pedal down, flat!"

62
REVELATION

The jagged outline of the church of St. Bridget sliced into the dark sky above, its silhouette merged into the burning, tormented village as flames and fireworks exchanged dominance. Buildings, including the warehouse and Whitby Rock shop, were in ruins. The pub spewed its patrons onto the street, and they stood under the swinging sign of the Wilson family coat of arms, the metallic finish of the serpent glowing as it reflected the twisting flames clawing at the night. The crowd looked on in silence and confusion.

Spud sat in the passenger seat, still in awe with the firework display. That was the best night of his life. In the back seat beside Jack, the case of cash and a dirt laden box of documents rattled against each other. They would head back to Jack's lockup; it would take them two hours. Crumb looked in the rear-view mirror, the sky now blistered with darting flame and bright yellow smoke, the marker left by the burning acetone.

"Wow, did you see that!" Crumb said. He took both hands off the steering wheel and then onto his head and ruffled his hair.

"That building, boom, it went up like a Roman candle!"

"You were lucky to get out of there."

"Careful, drive cool, you know!" Said Jack.

"Did you see the guys who were chasing me?"

"I saw the building come down on top of them!" Said Spud.

"The three of them? Do you think they got out?"

"Not sure. The entire roof came down on them all. All three."

"After we drop these off, you will need to get me back to the hotel. If the building buried those guys, then no-one knows I had anything to do with this. Except Peters. I need to get to him to find out what is going on. I got a text from Bob. He and Chris are OK and back at the Hotel, they have not seen or heard from Peters yet though."

The three make the round trip in just eight hours. They returned Jack to the hotel early morning as the group prepared to depart. As he arrived, Ken's executive coach parked and already loading in front of the hotel. Jack skipped up the steps and stopped at reception. The receptionist looked flustered.

"Hello there, checking out?"

"Oh, yes, I have just got to get my bags from the room."

"I just need your keys; the professor has taken care of all the paperwork. Did you enjoy your stay?"

"Yes, it was very eventful. I learned a lot. Before I go, I need to say bye to Peters, do you have his room number?"

"Peters?"

"Yes, you know, that old guy who sits in the Deck. At the window table."

"Sorry, the Deck is closed this morning; the kitchen staff have not arrived today. I am not sure what is going on. But Peters? I think you mean Ed?"

"Ed?"

"Yes, Ed. That is his name, Ed. He is the owner of the hotel. He does not have a room here. He is a delightful man though, a proper gentleman."

"But he is always in the Deck! He told us his name was Peters, and that he was staying here."

"Hmm, I know, that was Ed, I know it was. I saw him talking to one of your party. He does not stay here though; sometimes he takes his meals here, that is why you see him in the Deck. And you say 'Peters'? I know Ed's surname is Peterson."

"Peterson? And he has never stayed here?"

"No, he does not stay here. He comes here and checks on the accounts with his wife. I think her name is Ray or something like that. We have spoken little."

"Was he here this morning?"

"Now you mention it, I have not seen him since yesterday when he left with Pit and Peet."

"Pit and Peet?"

"Yes, you know them they are the Chef and the server in the Deck. I have not seen all three since last night."

Jack returned to his room, Russ has packed up and taken the stack of snacks, leaving two Whitby Rock candies on the side table. Jack grabbed them together with his backpack, before repositioning the chair in its place at the desk. He returned to reception and handed in his key. Jack stepped out of the hotel and made his way to the bus.

"They were all in on this, all of them." Jack said to himself as he turned to the hotel before he climbed onto the bus.

"All aboard then? Home we go. Might need a few stops. Flavorful hot curry last night." Said Ken, closing the bus door and sounding the horn.

63
FOUND

What is the quality that holds one character higher than another? Is it the actions that are chosen over those that are not? Is it the sacrifice made to protect others?

Wednesday, March 11th, 1998, Peters stood on tiptoes and peered out of the third-floor dormer window of his attic apartment in Hull, England. From high on the corner of Subway Street and Hessle Road the room was small, furnished with little furniture. The glass was dirty; he rubbed on the pane with the back of his hand, expecting it would clean the surface. Applying his worn flesh had no effect; the dirt was on the other side of the glass. Through the unmoved grime he could still get a decent view over the adjacent industrial yards and in the distance, Albert Dock.

His mind wandered to the past and his life with Rei. The times they had spent together in the war were often in his mind. Peters missed the excitement of smuggling and the freedom that he had enjoyed running around the country, being a step ahead of those that were always trying to catch them. Without Rei, he was lost. He missed their daughter and granddaughter, but he would see them soon. He had made sure they were taken care of, depositing money in the graveyard in Lysekil when he had the opportunity.

A line of condensation formed and ran down the inside of the window, almost touching his nose and connecting to a tear on its tip. It was Wednesday lunchtime, the commercial yards were quiet for an hour, containers stacked and prepared for loading. Peters considered the night of the robbery and demolition of the Whitby Rock warehouse. He had been in hiding since that time; it was what had brought him to this point; he was tired and time to go home, back to Sweden.

Peters had returned to Sneaton Thorpe with Pit and Peet the night of the robbery. His plan with the students was just a distraction, a setup, he had not counted on them making an escape. The idea was for the failed exchange to take attention away from the warehouse so he could make his way there alone. That did not happen, he did not think that the meeting would take place in the warehouse, it should have happened at the Wilson Arms.

When he arrived in Sneaton Thorpe, they all ended at the warehouse. That is when he found Ricky dealing with Jack. That was not what he had planned. Peters made his way into the production room to get to his formula and a few samples just as the explosions started. He escaped through the rear of the warehouse with what he went there to get. It was not until later that he found the students had escaped with the money and some of his documents. Because he ran, the Society had implicated him with the whole robbery, and he needed to stay low. That is when he came to Hull.

He knew the Society would not give up trying to find him, even after the five long years since he had fled to his hideout. The small apartment on Hessle Road was something that he had kept in his back pocket since he came to England. A safe house. Now it was his refuge, no one knew he had it, not even his family. He had remained quiet and hidden, but five years was long enough.

After the Whitby Rock robbery, he had got a message to his daughter, Pippi, in Lysekil, telling her to move away with his granddaughter, maybe to Norway. She had links there through her mother, Rei. He thought of his wife and played with the wedding ring that was always in his grasp, within his jacket pocket; he sewed it in there by loose stitching. The ring turned between his fingers. Memories of how they first met, saving each other all those years ago. Peters missed her.

His plan was to stay in hiding until he thought it safe to get back to Sweden. Today was the day that he would make it out of England. Berthed in the Albert Docks was a freighter bound for Gothenburg later that night. That would be his transport home. Peters knew one of the crew, a friend that he had made when he first arrived in Hull in 1965, and they had secured passage for him on the boat.

He gathered his belongings into a backpack, nothing more than clothing and a shaving kit. He stuffed a handful of Whitby Rock candies, a sample of what he could make, into his jacket pocket, and left the apartment to make his way to the boat. Subway Street connected to Albert Dock by a footpath. Peters' route would take him beside the industrial storage yards that backed onto the path. High chain-link fences topped with razor wire protected the shipping containers from intruders. The walk would take him fifteen minutes at the most, he had plenty of time.

Peters thought nothing of it as he passed a break in the fence with an open shipping container positioned behind. The salt air from the docks hit his face, and he felt his skin tighten as if an astringent had been applied. He took a deep breath; the cold air burned the back of his throat. The sky was a light blue; it felt like Spring. A gull squawked and its silhouette lifted into the sky in front of him. He looked up to follow it. At that moment, everything went dark for him. A blackout hood forced over his head, he felt hands grip both of his arms, holding them to his side. He was no match for their strength as they bundled him into a van parked within the container.

64
SOCIETY

What is it to be a member of a society, all secret to others? To associate with other determined individuals, all arrayed in common criminal enterprise. Small, purposeful groups are for the great majority of people a way towards success and gratification. But to cross or betray them leads to a pathway of darker intent. The Order of St. Bridget, an organized group of criminal activity that has been in place for centuries and still has its members at hand, may be such a society.

It was 5:40 a.m. on Thursday, March 12th, 1998. A full moon waited in the sky for the sun to rise. At its peak in thirty minutes, the moon was an unstoppable countdown for a final resolution. Small grains within a large glass hourglass turned thirty minutes prior, formed shifting pyramids that rose and dissipated in alternating cycles as the sand poured through the narrow opening at its center.

"You recall your oath? The one you took in 1965 when you landed here?" said Ricky, holding the hourglass above his head, in view of all within sight. Ricky Wilson was the landlord of the Wilson Arms and had survived the explosion in the Whitby Rock warehouse in 1992. He stood together with Pit on his right and Peet holding a bell pull with both hands. Above them, tied with a single loop of the rope around his leg, hanging upside down was Ed Peterson, 'Peters'. Held in the bell chamber of St. Bridget's church in Sneaton Thorpe, where it began.

"The oath of the Order you took with us all together, in this place, and I repeat it for you now, in case you forget."

"I with an earnest soul in its most forthright motion, promise and swear, that I will with true allegiance, always commend, forever shelter, and never expose, any of the actions, trades or industry of the Society, bearing under no less a forfeiture than suffocation of my soul, and thus if proven having my body presented, pointing towards the eternal burning damnation of purgatory, in a place hallowed to this order of Saint Bridget and at time of a full moon."

"What you did those years ago almost killed us all. And you must face the consequence."

"Your accomplices destroyed our operation here and pushed it into the light of the law."

"You have been running, but now we have caught you, and you will pay the price. And so will all of your family and those who have profited from your scheme."

"You, will never find them, I have ensured that." Said Peters.

"I helped all three of you when we arrived here."

"You had nothing when we got off the boat in Hull. I got you new identities. Gus, I gave you the pub here. Erik, and Josef you had it good at the hotel. I made the process.

I designed the factory. we paid the debt and more. You all took that from me. I did not break the oath you all did!"

"You were an old man then. You are now extinct and so are your exploits. Nobody cares what you did during the war. Yes, the debt was paid, but that was long ago. The hotel could not handle the volume, it was time for us to move on. Without you." Said Gus.

"We have removed everything from the graves, all the cash. But the recipe and all the documents disappeared. Someone has it. And we will find them."

"The moon is at its full and then will wane, which you will not live to see."

Gus took a large silver chalice, engraved with the Wilson coat of arms on its side. Reverend Coombs brought in a bowl of water and blessed it before he poured water into the chalice, so that it was half full. Pit pushed a step ladder to be beside Peters, Gus followed.

"It is the end, Ed, this is the end, for you."

In the nave, from the congregation, a chanted prayer.

"Guide us through this abyss of compassion and pity and grant me us the strength to put goodness to one side and beg fortune and deliverance the thief who has betrayed."

Pit took hold of Peter's jacket and pulled it down over his arms, so it held them immobile. A few Whitby Rock candies fell from the upturned pockets and scattered as they hit the stone floor below. Peet placed all his weight on the pull rope. The bell turned and gave out a solitary chime. Gus took the chalice and held it up to Peters' head and raised it until the water inside covered his nose and mouth. Peters tried to twist and raise his head, he spluttered. Held there, upside down, for half an hour. He had little strength left. Water spilled onto the floor. As the new moon met its full phase, the struggle with death ended. Life left the now limp body, and it hung in place, and found there later that same morning.

Gus and Pit climbed down the ladder and Pit removed it to the van waiting outside. Peet remained in position until the other two were ready to depart, then let go of the pull to release the bell. The sound of the chimes followed the van out of the village. It was ten past six, and the moon was at its fullest. The witness congregation returned to their homes.

65
ST. BRIDGET

S ometimes, just as you give up hope, a feather from the wing of a passing angel floats into your hand and provides an opportunity that you did not expect.

Detective Inspector Hunter had exhausted all leads. The true identity of the hanging man was still a mystery. The facts pointed to a link to Sweden, but nothing had formed. Maybe the wedding ring belonged to someone the man knew and wanted to remember, maybe his wife. Hunter had studied the test results for the 'WHITBY ROCK' candy and compared them together with the contents of PC Johnstone's stomach. The chemical composition from each matched. However, PC Johnstone's digestive system had ten times the quantity of the hallucinogenic compounds found in the single candy. That explained why the irrational Johnstone had acted as he had when he made the platform from the hymn books and climbed the rope.

It was May 1st, 1998, now almost fifty days since the day of the incident. There was nothing she could think of that would push the investigation further at any speed. She needed her regular coffee and to think. Before she left her desk, Hunter pulled the St. Bridget case files together into a neat pile. There was another case that she would need to look at, part of a new investigation team. She required the desk space to examine those files. Disappointed that the leads had gone cold, Hunter wandered through the corridor to the break room. She gazed down at her shoes as she walked and listened to her own footsteps echoing on the tiled floor. Her shoes polished to a mirror finish. A thought from her childhood flickered for a moment but dissipated as she entered the break room. The room was empty. She sat at the small table to consider her actions for a moment and stared at the microwave. The glass door exhibited more fingerprints than a crime scene. The entire space was filthy. Did no one clean up in this place? She washed and filled her cup with fresh coffee, then headed back to her office.

As Hunter sat down at her desk and pulled her chair forward, a stack of documents held within plastic see-though folders piled together in the center. Administration had marked the pile for her attention. She turned the first and held it closer, enough to allow her desk lamp to illuminate the contents through the glare of the plastic. An envelope already opened; its contents separated into three different clear plastic covers.

Addressed to Detective Hunter of the North Yorkshire Police Service. Hunter looked at the postage stamps. They bore an abstract modern-art type of image and the word SVERIGE, postmarked 'POSTEN, SVERIGE'. Imprinted along their center was a date, March 14th, 1998. Two days after the St. Bridget incident.

Her grip released the first and as it fell back onto her desk, exchanged it for the second, an unfolded letter. A handwritten note on what felt like, from its weight, heavy bond paper. She glanced at the third, remaining on her desk was a well-worn and pressed extract from a newspaper article. The newsprint appeared faded and smudged. She could not understand what the heading meant 'Tre Unga Män Försvann' but could see that the article identified the year as 1965, the rest was in Swedish, she guessed. She would send the page for translation. Her attention now focused on the delicate handwriting of the letter, which was in English.

Hunter took a breath and read it to herself, her lips moved to the words without voice:

'Dear Detective,'

'You are now reading this letter because you have found my body. More likely hanging in St. Bridget's Church in Sneaton Thorpe. If that is the case, then they have murdered me. Now I will tell you all about how this happened. You must find them before they reach my family.'

Detective inspector Hunter knew that the following information could provide the missing parts if she was fortunate enough. She continued.

'My name is Edelborg Peterson. I am known as Ed or as Peters to those who meet me. I lived in Sweden. Something connected me to the events that are in the attached article, you will see. These things made me to come to England in 1965 with the three disappeared men. They were Gus Neilson, Erik and Josef Holm, brothers. We were all involved in smuggling things between Gothenburg and Hull, things that made money. I needed money to support my family. We all landed together. Soon we moved near to

Whitby because the boss had his primary operation there. It was the mushroom growing warehouse in Sneaton Thorpe. We were to help move the candy drugs to other places on the boats.'

'When we arrived there, we were first taken to the St. Bridget's church and made to take the oath to be into the Society. The Society of St. Bridget they are who have killed me now. I had an idea to make an LSD from extract of the mushrooms and because I am a chemical engineer, we did it. I worked on the process and we set up the Whitby Rock factory. It worked very well. We used the Great Eastern hotel and the Wilson Arms pub to wash the money.'

'Gus changed his name to Ricky, Erik to Peet, and Josef to Pit. I became Peters. Some weeks I would return to Lysekil to see my daughter when we organized shipments there, but we could not talk. We did this for a long time until they said I was too old, and they would push me out of the business in 1992. I knew they had a big money exchange, so I got some help, and we planned to take the money and the recipe documents. There is more money hidden under the three graves in the graveyard at St. Bridget.'

'They knew it was me soon after the robbery we did, and I could not collect all the recipe and cash. I had to run, hiding in Hull.'

'That is all I need to say, you can connect the rest.'

'Ed Peterson.'

66
HUNT

This information returned the St. Bridget's case file back into the center of Hunter's desk. She tore off the brown elastic band that held the contents secure, the papers and photographs spilled like the guts of a slaughtered animal over her desk. Hunter logged into her computer and created a memo request; her frenzied fingers could not keep up with the words and thoughts in her head.

Hunter wrote the department request Interpol issue a black alert. A black alert is a request that seeks information on unidentified bodies. The letter provided detail and maybe a corroboration of the identity of the man found in the bell tower, but not yet any formal evidence for confirmation of a name. Hunter also requested to go to Sweden to make a direct enquiry for information that the Swedish National Police Board may hold on Edelborg Peterson.

In the meantime, Hunter would revisit Sneaton Thorpe and speak with the Reverend and others to test their recollections of what happened against their original statements. The Great Eastern Hotel? The same hotel that she had roomed the day of the event. She would also need to visit the Wilson Arms. This would need some resources. Hunter called her team to meet.

The investigation would continue, and she set to travel to Sneaton Thorpe the next day. On her arrival, she parked her car beside the entrance gate to St. Bridget's church. The place where PC Johnstone had parked his car on the fateful day of the incident. Hunter sat in her vehicle for a moment and considered the church to her right. The spire appeared smaller than she remembered and the graveyard greener. She pulled the interview files from the case folder on the passenger seat and made for the vicarage to speak with Reverend Coombes. The residence was five minutes at walking pace from the church, so the statement made by Coombes showed.

She arrived at the vicarage and the small wooden gate within the weathered picket fence, Hunter checked her time. It had taken her just under the five minutes. She found the latch on the gate and pushed it to allow the gate to open onto a brick paved pathway to the front door of the vicarage. A royal blue paneled door with a heavy brass knocker at its center. Hunter gave it a couple of raps and after a few seconds the door opened.

"Hello." A small balding man dressed in the attire of a vicar greeted Hunter as she stood on the doorstep. It was not Reverend Coombes. She held her badge towards the man's ruddy face as she replied. His eyes crossed as he read it.

"Oh, Hello. I am Detective Inspector Hunter. And I am looking for Reverend Coombes."

"Reverend Coombes? He is no longer at this parish. I am Reverend Harrison."

"Reverend Coombes left?"

"Well, he disappeared. You had better come in and I can explain better."

Hunter accepted the invitation and followed Harrison to the lounge and a comfortable chair.

"Tea?"

"A coffee if you have one, please."

"I'm sure we can arrange that. Sugar?"

"No thank you, just a splash of milk please."

Harrison left for the kitchen; Hunter took the time to scan Coombes' statement again. She needed to clear up several issues. Coffee now in hand, Hunter started her questions, making notes as she did so. The coffee was good.

"You are Reverend Harrison?"

"Yes, John Harrison."

"How long have you been the vicar here?"

"Well, they appointed me just last week."

"Last week? But what happened to Reverend Coombes, you said that he disappeared?"

"Yes. We don't know, he just left with no warning. Most of his belongings left here too."

"Do you know what date that was?"

"I'm told that it was the end of March, no one knows the exact date."

"There has been no contact with him since?"

"Not to my knowledge."

"Ok. Do you have a contact for the church, the administration?"

"Yes, I can get you that."

"We also need to check the phone records for the number at the church, can you let me have that?"

"The phone at the church? There is no phone at the church, only here at the vicarage."

"No phone at the church. Ever?"

"No, there is no phone or line at the church. Not to my knowledge anyway."

After a few additional questions and some pleasantries, Hunter left the vicarage, her coffee half finished. She had more questions now than the answers that she had received. Hunter returned to her car and examined the statement made by Coombes. She read the sentence, 'It was about 6:30 then. I entered the nave and then went to the bell chamber where the body was hanging. That is when I called the police.' He did not say that he had called the police from the church, only that he had called the police, setting the time at that point, but not the location.

Hunter scanned towards the large oak tree in the graveyard, to the setting of the three graves disturbed the night of the incident, only now there were no headstones to mark their location and the church had reinstated the ground. Her team was getting an order in place to excavate that area, a location suggested by Peterson's letter that held buried proceeds. She suspected that the group had extracted anything previously buried in those locations already.

Replacing the statements back into the folder, Hunter made her way to the Wilson Arms. She passed the rubble of a demolished building on her right. Hunter guessed it was the remains of the Whitby Rock warehouse and shop. She approached the Wilson Arms and noticed as she got closer the windows and doors shuttered and boarded. A notice on the main door confirmed that the business had closed, the sign above moved and creaked in the breeze. She questioned a passerby who told her that the pub had been closed since the end of March, the same day that Reverend Coombes disappeared.

The last visit of the day would be to the Great Eastern Hotel in Scarborough. It was getting late and she could get a room there if she needed. The route to Scarborough took her along the coast and her mind traveled back in time to when she was a child and the excitement the view brought, a stay at the seaside with her new family.

She arrived at the hotel after a forty-minute drive. She looked up the steps to the entrance door. The Great Easter Hotel was closed, there was no sign of activity.

67
WEB

uilt upon a series of sequential waves joined by the ever present but invisible rhythm of the universe, events continue forward. A pattern determined by mathematical fractal, like the shape of the waves it molds into form. History destined to repeat itself; unable to take an alternative path. Because there is none to take as it sets the outcome.

The request to Interpol and the Swedish Police had confirmed details and corroborated the identity of the body. Detective Hunter and her team had visited Gothenburg and had amassed evidence linking the events to the St. Bridget incident. It had been over three years since Hunter had stepped into the church to find the body hanging from the rope.

The investigation had found that the handwritten letter signed by Peterson was most likely genuine. Fingerprints identified on the paper and envelope confirmed a match with the body. The evidence provided many leads, and like a spider's web not only captured the perpetrators but connected to locations and persons not yet discovered.

The police had established that the identity of the body was most likely to be that of Edelborg Peterson. However, they had not located his daughter, Pippi, or his granddaughter Freda. It was suspected that they had travelled to Norway where they had some connection, but they could find no trace of their whereabouts. Evidence uncovered that a criminal group had established a drug smuggling route between Lysekil, Gothenburg, Hull, and Whitby. That investigation was ongoing.

68
CALM

U p to this point, the day of 19th of July 2002, ten years since the Whitby Rock robbery, had absorbed Jack in thought about much. That was not uncommon. He preferred to allow his mind to wander, to play, to plan and to strategize about all around him. But at this moment his thoughts were sporadic and without organization. He needed to settle his mind; something to analyze.

He stared out at the calm Florida lagoon in front of him. The surface of the water captured the blue sky above and held it as an accomplice in a mirror image. In his eyes a reflection in miniature that represented the whole, a painted study of the unfolding event.

Now in his late thirties, he had aged well over the years and appeared younger to others as they first met him. Jack stood against the window of his waterfront office, as still as a heron waiting for its prey. Viewed from outside, a shadow, dressed in a dark suit and black pressed dress shirt, a silver watch at his wrist. His appearance was the archetypal example of privilege. A description attributed and used by many without thought or knowledge of what process had delivered the bearer to this time and to this place.

For most of his life, Jack practiced living in the present, the now. He tried hard to accomplish this, but unguarded thoughts allowed tendrils of his previous existence to reach into his mind and pull him to think of times before. There was no desire to go back to those events. Why should he? The journey to this point had gone, no will could change that and the many obstacles he had overcome on the way. It was easy to understand, he thought, that the only circumstance that anyone should spend effort to consider should be the moment that met the end. That was not now, was it? He questioned himself.

As always, and as was his wont, he forced his mind to a time ahead and moved on, imagined what will be, eager to construct visual narratives of the future. He was to have greater success; and he meant it; he planned it, but maybe it would be on a different schedule. The tendril grasped and probed and then halted him again in thought. He waited, not with any anticipation or apprehension of what he deserved, but now conscious that his world was about to change. Just as the tide would change, as it reflected in the morphing composition in his eyes as he continued to gaze on the waterfront. A thought extracted to his mind came into focus. Made some time ago without reason, a debt had now become payable. He sighed; it was true the debt was due.

The organized office in which he stood had little in the way of furniture, and that is how he had designed it. A desk, a chair, and a small set of drawers. His desktop was bereft of clutter save a triple arrangement of flat screens, a keyboard, a mouse, a phone, a face mask, and a single picture postcard. The walls of the office held, at precise composition, several framed prints of different locations including an English fishing village. Various images a throwback to different but familiar places and times. Moments of many events of the past, neither to be the start nor any beginning.

Jack remained there, between his desk and the full height windows, and studied more. The tendrils encroached into his mind again. They pulled his thoughts in many directions, but he knew they had a purpose.

The palm of his right hand rested upright on the glazing. He pressed his fingers hard into the glass, hoping a physical connection would return his mind to today, to the solution. Resisted by the flat surface, his fingerprints left smears on the pane, like miniature rainbows; the glass was always warm to the touch, warmer than the air-conditioned office. For a moment, the transparent smoothness connected him to the outside world, to the present and to the twenty degrees of separation that the air conditioning kept.

His view encapsulated the entire extent of the dock and the adjacent walkway and parking area. The walkway, a wooden deck with a handrail on the waterside, led from the dock to the boat ramp and parking lot. There was no movement or activity other than the undulating bobbing of the various boats.

Jack looked down on to the water and at the multi-colored reflections that moved along in regular precession. Their frequency timed to his breathing as they lapped onto the seawall. The tide was changing. The carpet of ripples collided into each other before they dissipated into nothing, ebbing away atop the boundary between water and air. Jack came back to the day; now aware, he considered the scene.

69
DELIVERY

The 'Magisk Keps' a yacht ten times the length of a family car, moored in open water away from the dock, anchored into the sea grass below. It was by far the largest boat amongst the others and was apparent from the size and category of the craft it was ocean-going. A Swedish maritime flag, a yellow cross on a blue background fluttered on its stern. It highlighted the boat may have made the three-week passage across the Atlantic to its current anchorage.

The brilliance of early afternoon sun reflected off the hull of the vessel and acted as a lens as it intensified the light in bright flashes. It was challenging, but possible to look at the boat, and through the haze and dazzle of reflections, make out a human form. Jack squinted his eyelids to enable him to pick out a single female figure, standing at the bow of the yacht. A slim silhouette upright against the blue water beyond. He knew her.

"There you are." He said to himself.

Jack refocused as the engine sound belonging to a small white van caught his attention as the vehicle flew into his view. The vehicle towed a small trailer which carried two identical jet skis that hung onto the back for dear life as the trailer swung back and forth. Loose gravel displaced and crunched under the momentum of the tires. In a single flowing movement, the van stopped, reversed at a speed much slower than the quickening of the van's high revving engine described, and then halted at the boat ramp. It was now in a position as close to the water as possible. Depositing its rear wheels and trailer on the angle of the ramp with the jet skis now part submerged, the water lapping at their bows.

The doors of the van opened in synchronicity. Two figures, both dressed in the same white overalls, made their way to the rear of the van. They took turns to each pull out a waterproof, molded case and throw the attached strap over their shoulder. In unison, they kicked off their footwear; the shoes landed beside the van. They floated the jet skis off the trailer and boarded, started, and launched towards the yacht. A plume of water sprayed high off each into the parking lot as they sped away. A third man picked up the shoes and threw them into the van before leaving the parking area at the same speed as they had arrived.

The female figure on the Magisk Keps turned in the activity's direction and gestured to the men in recognition. Not a wave, but a pre-established sequence of hand movements. Jack knew what they meant. The jet skis cut through the water side by side together towards their target.

The desk phone shook, a sharp ring vibrated the handset in its seat. Jack turned away from the window, startled for a moment. The caller identification screen illuminated in a green light as the phone received the call. He decided not to answer. The number on the display was the one he expected, but there was something he had to think of first, something from his past, something embedded. A tendril from his subconscious hooked into a memory, twisting, and turning it into view.

He thought of his childhood, his choices, the days at work, meeting Angie and that week in Scarborough. Now he was here, waiting to choose.

70
DISCOVERY

D rawing parallel lines in the lagoon's surface, the wake of each jet ski converged on the 'Magic Caps' at the same time. The two men climbed on board with their cases. Standing close to his window, Jack signed from his office to Angie, still standing on the bow of the boat.

"All well there?"

"Yes, all good here. We have the parcels. I will call you later for dinner."

Jack turned away from the window and made his way to his desk. As he plonked himself in his high-backed leather chair, it crumpled and formed around his frame. Creases worn in place by years of use met like old friends and creaked as they did so. In front of him a picture postcard, a nighttime image of Bayside, Miami. The amber glow of waterfront restaurants spilling on to the marina set against the stark concrete and glass high-rise apartments and hotels of Biscayne Boulevard.

He turned the card and read the message on the rear for the tenth time, then turned it again to view the image on its front.

'My father told me all about you. I hope to meet you soon. As you know, we have business to conclude.'

Signed Pippi Peterson.

"Business to conclude. Yes, we do, Miss Peterson."

He pulled his desk phone close and scrolled through the menu until the caller identification screen displayed the number that he wanted, one that had called him earlier. He dialed and waited.

A phone rang as it sat face up on a table at a waterfront bar and restaurant. A lone woman in her 40s, blond shoulder length hair, played with a handwritten letter and a newspaper cutting. She picked up the phone and checked the caller identification before answering, gazing into the amber glow of the marina in front of her. It held the same view as on the postcard sitting in Jack's hand.

"Hello there, Jack." The post card spun in Jack's fingers to allow him to re-read the message again.

"Hello Pippi. You found me."

"Yes, we need to meet, don't you think?"

"Yes, we should meet. I need to explain to you what happened. With your father."

"I know what happened, you need to know what is happening now."

A pair of binoculars, held steady on the rail of a tenth story balcony of a nearby hotel, repositioned themselves and focused on Pippi as she engaged in the telephone conversation.